PADDINGTON
Takes to TV

YEARLING BOOKS are designed especially to entertain and enlighten young people. The finest available books for children have been selected under the direction of Charles F. Reasoner, Professor of Elementary Education, New York University.

For a complete listing of all Yearling titles,
write to Education Sales Department, Dell Publishing Co., Inc.,
1 Dag Hammarskjold Plaza, New York, N.Y. 10017

PADDINGTON
Takes to TV

MICHAEL BOND

Illustrated by IVOR WOOD

A YEARLING BOOK

Published by
Dell Publishing Co., Inc.
1 Dag Hammarskjold Plaza
New York, New York 10017

Yearling ® TM 913705, Dell Publishing Co., Inc.

ISBN: 0-440-45930-3

Reprinted by arrangement with Houghton Mifflin Company
Printed in the United States of America
Seventh Dell Printing—April 1979

CW

CONTENTS

"To Blue Peter and all who sail in her"

Some years ago, when I was a television cameraman with the British Broadcasting Corporation, I sometimes worked on a programme called "Blue Peter."

"Blue Peter" is one of the most popular children's programmes on British Television. Val, John, Peter and Lesley are the hosts, and together they visit unusual places, show how to make things, organise wildly successful campaigns to help the needy, keep various pets and generally cause quiet to descend on the living-rooms of Britain for twenty-five minutes or so every Monday and Thursday afternoon.

Somewhere along the line Paddington started to get involved too. In the beginning it was once a year with a story specially written for the "Blue Peter Annual"; now, in a repeat showing as it were, the first seven stories are gathered together to make up PADDINGTON'S BLUE PETER STORY BOOK, as the book was originally titled in England, or as PADDINGTON TAKES TO TV as it is known in the United States.

Michael Bond

PADDINGTON
Takes to TV

Paddington
Takes the Cake

"Paddington's won a prize in a Blue Peter competition?" Mr Brown lowered his newspaper and stared across the breakfast table.

"Don't look so surprised, Henry," said Mrs Brown. "He only heard this morning."

"There was a letter from the Editor congratulating him," exclaimed Jonathan.

"*And* a super recipe for a Christmas cake from Val," added Judy.

"A Christmas cake!" Mr Brown looked for a moment as if his bacon and eggs had suddenly developed a nasty taste. "I hope he's not going to try it out on us."

"I doubt if we shall be allowed within a mile of it," said Mrs Brown reassuringly. "It's all part of the competition. Apparently the six winners have all been invited to bake a cake and take it along to the television studio."

"They all get a Christmas hamper," said Jonathan, "but the one who makes the best cake gets a special prize of his own choice."

"That's a dangerous thing to say when Paddington's around," said Mr Brown. "If he wins we shall be living on marmalade for the rest of our lives."

"Val showed all the ingredients in a programme some weeks ago," said Judy. "There were some close-ups of the raisins and sultanas and she asked the viewers to guess how many there were in each pile. Paddington was watching at the time but I didn't dream he'd go in for it."

"Where's he going to make this cake?" asked Mr Brown with interest.

"In the garden if I have anything to do with it," broke in Mrs Bird sternly. With memories of some of Paddington's previous attempts at cooking still fresh in her mind the Browns' housekeeper intended putting her foot down at an early stage in the proceedings. "I'm not having him in my kitchen. With Christmas just around the corner I've enough to do as it is."

"Have some more toast, Henry," said Mrs Brown, hastily changing the subject.

In point of fact only a few minutes before she had offered Paddington the use of an old field kitchen which Mr Brown kept at the back of his shed and normally only brought out when they went camping, but she had a nasty feeling in the back of her mind that her generous gesture might not meet with universal approval.

"I expect he'll find somewhere to do it," she said vaguely. "You know Paddington. He usually does. He's that sort of bear."

14

Paddington ha
order to cor
let he wa
It
he

The door to the Browns' garage slowly opened and a moment later some familiar looking whiskers, followed by an equally familiar hat, appeared in the gap as their owner stood peering round the garden with a guilty expression on his face.

Having made sure that all was well Paddington disappeared from view again, closing the doors behind him with a loud click.

A few seconds later a strange rumbling sound broke the stillness of the morning air. It was a sound not unlike that of an aircraft revving up its engines, and one which Mrs Bird would have recognised immediately had she been there, but fortunately for her peace of mind the Browns' housekeeper was busy helping the rest of the family finish off their Christmas shopping.

However, if the noise outside the garage was loud, inside it was almost deafening. In fact it was so loud that

d to pull his hat well down over his ears in
centrate at all on the important looking book-
s trying to read.

was a small, but brighly coloured volume, and it was
ded YOUR SPIN DRIER – OPERATING INSTRUCTIONS.

Drawing up an old box, Paddington settled himself
down, dipped his paw into a nearby jar of marmalade, and
began to read.

Gradually however, his face dropped and his whiskers
began to sag, for although as a book it was quite interesting, he soon decided that like most other instruction
manuals he'd come across in the past it dealt with practically every kind of situation except the one he wanted.

The first two or three pages were devoted to telling the
owner how lucky she was, and this was followed by a
number of pictures showing a happy, laughing housewife
standing beside a mountain of freshly dried sheets, while
outside the kitchen window a storm appeared to be raging
and all her neighbour's washing hung limp and sodden
on a line.

Paddington went through the booklet several times in
case he'd missed something by mistake, but although it
devoted pages and pages to the drying of towels, sheets,
blankets, woollens and various other items, as far as he
could make out it didn't so much as mention the possi-
bility of using the machine for making cakes of any sort
let alone Christmas ones.

Giving vent to a loud sigh he closed the book and
turned his attention back to his immediate surroundings.

When Val had demonstrated cake-making on Blue
Peter it had all seemed remarkably easy and she had left
the studio looking spotlessly clean, with scarcely a trace of

flour anywhere, whereas glancing around at the mess in Mr Brown's garage even Paddington had to admit that matters couldn't have been worse.

Paddington didn't believe in doing things by halves and he'd poured some extremely generous helpings of ingredients into Mrs Brown's washing-up bowl, multiplying Val's instructions at least six times over before adding the milk and water with the aid of a watering can.

It was when he'd come to stir the mixture that his troubles had started. Having bent several of Mrs Bird's best spoons without even moving it he'd tried his paw with Mr Brown's electric paint stirrer instead. But even this device had begun to emit clouds of black smoke in protest, and when he'd withdrawn it hastily before it caught fire it had suddenly burst into life again, scattering

dough in all directions.

It was then, when matters seemed at their lowest ebb, that he'd had the bright idea of using Mrs Bird's spin drier.

Placing the instruction book carefully on one side before it got too many stains on its pages, Paddington crossed the garage to where the machine stood heaving and groaning in the middle of the floor.

Switching it off at the wall point, he waited while the drum inside slowed down and gradually came to a stop, then he reached forward with a paw and cautiously lifted the lid. As he did so Paddington suddenly stiffened, and for a moment he stood rooted to the spot, his eyes opening wider and wider. Then, after pinching himself several times in order to make sure he wasn't dreaming, he threw back the lid and peered inside the now silent machine.

Admittedly there were still a few traces of cake mixture left clinging to the sides of the drum, particularly around the edge of the holes which lined it, but apart from one or two of the larger chunks of fruit which he'd put in for luck, the main bulk of the cake had almost completely disappeared.

Paddington rubbed his eyes and was about to consult the instruction booklet once again in case there was a section dealing with disappearing contents when he felt something wet and sticky land on his foot.

He glanced down and then nearly fell over backwards with astonishment, for there, sticking to his fur, was a large lump of the missing mixture. Worse still, from a pipe low down in the side of the machine, more was appearing with every passing second.

After poking a screwdriver hopefully up the waste pipe

Paddington began taking the machine to pieces while he considered ways and means of breaking the news to Mrs Bird that several pounds of Christmas cake mixture was firmly lodged between the drum of her spin drier and the outside case.

Paddington wasn't the sort of bear who gave up easily in the face of difficulties. All the same, he looked most relieved when he'd got the machine back together again, particularly when he found he'd been able to salvage almost a bowlful of the cake mixture into the bargain.

In her talk on Blue Peter, Val had mentioned having to bake her cake for a matter of several hours, but with time rapidly running out Paddington decided not to take any chances, and after placing the bowl of mixture inside Mr Brown's oven – which was really little more than a large metal box in the shape of a biscuit tin – he lit the burners underneath and carefully adjusted them to give the maximum amount of heat.

Soon the smell of freshly baking cake began to waft across the garage and he licked his lips in anticipation as he approached the oven in order to inspect his handiwork.

In the past Paddington had often noticed that one disaster was frequently followed by a second. Even so, with all his previous experience, he was still unprepared for the sight which met his eyes when he opened the oven door.

Letting go of the handle he collapsed onto the garage floor and stared at the oven with a mournful expression on his face, for the cake, far from looking golden brown and ready to ice like the one Val had shown on television, had risen so high and grown so wide it filled every nook and cranny, barely leaving room for the wisps of smoke it was giving off, let alone leaving space for anything to lever it out with.

Paddington was accustomed to things looking black on the outside, but from where he was sitting they looked unusually black on the inside as well. So black, he couldn't for the moment see even the faintest chink of light to relieve the gloom.

The Commissionaire on duty outside the BBC Television Centre looked in through the window of Paddington's taxi.

"'ave you an appointment, sir?" he asked.

Paddington raised his hat politely. "I've come about the cake," he announced importantly.

The Commissionaire exchanged glances with a second man who had just joined him. "I wish them builders would hurry up," he said, nodding towards some half-finished studios nearby. "Can't hear a thing for their blessed pneumatic drills. I thought for a moment this young gentleman said he'd come about a cake!"

"I won a prize," shouted Paddington, trying to make himself heard above the din. "I counted all the raisins."

The Commissionaire rubbed his chin thoughtfully. The inside of the taxi appeared to be littered with an incredible amount of bits and pieces. Next to the driver there was an enormous box labelled BLUE PETER. HANDLE WITH CARE. THIS SIDE UP. whilst apart from Paddington, the back seat was covered with bits and pieces including a number of half eaten sandwiches, an old suitcase and what looked like a large jar of marmalade.

Suddenly his face cleared. "Raisins," he said. "I expect you'll be wanting the gentleman in charge of Current Affairs."

He turned to his colleague and nodded significantly. "They wants a bit of understanding some of these foreigners," he said. "Probably one of them explorers just got back from overseas. Been collecting wild animals for the Blue Peter programme most likely. We'd best get this stuff sent along to the studio before anything happens to it."

He signalled some nearby porters to pick up the luggage and then turned to Paddington with renewed respect.

"You come along with me, sir," he said, leading the way through some imposing glass doors. "I'll take you up to see 'is nibs straight away."

"Take me up to see his nibs!" exclaimed Paddington, looking most surprised as he followed the man into a lift.

Although he'd promised to tell the Browns all about his visit to the Television Centre he certainly hadn't bargained on being asked to write it all down. But before he had time to even consider the matter he found himself being whisked along a corridor near the top of the building and into a carpeted room which looked out high over the London rooftops.

As the Commissionaire bowed himself out a tall, distinguished looking man rose from behind a desk and advanced across the room. "Good afternoon," he said. "I'm H.E.C.A.D."

"Oh, dear," said Paddington. He wiped his paw carefully on the back of his duffle coat before holding it out. "I'm sorry to hear that. I hope you'll be better soon."

"It's not an illness," said the man stiffly. "It's a job." He gazed rather distastefully at an old marmalade chunk which seemd to have found its way onto his hand. "I'm Head of Expeditions – Current Affairs Division."

"I'm afraid I didn't quite catch your name," he continued, as he riffled through some papers on his desk.

"It's Brown," said Paddington. "Paddington Brown."

"Brown . . . Brown . . . " The man repeated it several times. "Er . . . how are things at UNO?" he asked.

"Where?" asked Paddington in surprise.

"UNO," repeated the Head of Expeditions.

"I'm afraid I don't know," said Paddington hotly. "Nobody's told me."

The Head of Expeditions ran a hand round his collar. "Perhaps you'd like to take a seat," he said, giving Paddington a strange look. "I won't keep you a moment."

So saying he disappeared through a door into the next room where a buzz of conversation broke out, followed by the sound of drawers being opened and shut.

The noise went on for quite a long time and then the

door opened again. "I suppose you wouldn't be the feller we sent to the Plain of Jars?" asked a voice hopefully.

Paddington hastily removed his paw from a pot of marmalade. "The Plain of Jars!" he exclaimed, looking most impressed. "I've never heard of there being a *plain* of jars before. Mrs Bird always makes me put mine in the dustbin."

The man took a deep breath. "The trouble is," he said, choosing his words with care, "we've got so many people on the go it's difficult to keep track of them all. I wonder if you'd mind telling me where you come from. We can't find any Brown on our records."

"I come from Peru," said Paddington doubtfully. "*Darkest* Peru, but . . . "

"Thank you," said the Head of Expeditions gratefully, as he disappeared again. "Thank you very much."

This time he was gone even longer, and as the clattering in the next room grew louder and the sound of furniture being moved added itself to the general hub-bub, Paddington began to look anxiously at a clock on the wall, which showed well past the time when Blue Peter was due to begin.

When the Head of Expeditions finally reappeared his tie was askew and he was joined by several other people who formed a small group in the doorway.

"I say, I'm awfully sorry," he began, looking rather embarrassed as he ran a hand through his hair. "We've just moved office and all our files seem to be mixed up. We can't find any trace of an expedition to South America, let alone Darkest Peru."

"Perhaps he's one of them Hottentots," said a cleaner helpfully, as he eyed Paddington from behind his broom.

"Either that or he wants a good shave."

"A Hottentot!" exclaimed Paddington, looking most offended. "I'm not a Hottentot – I'm a bear!"

"I've come all the way from number thirty-two Windsor Gardens," he continued, as the others stared at him in the silence which followed, "and I've brought my cake for the Blue Peter competition. Mrs Bird's going to be most upset if she doesn't see me!"

Peter Purves slipped a handkerchief from his trouser pocket and glanced across at John and Val as he dabbed at his forehead.

Things hadn't gone at all well that afternoon. First there had been the mysterious non-arrival of one of the competitors in the Christmas Cake competition. Annoyingly, it had been the owner of the best cake there. The one that undoubtedly deserved to win first prize.

Then there had been a rather nasty disturbance a few seconds before. It had all taken place somewhere behind the lights so that it had been difficult to make out exactly what was going on, but he'd distinctly noticed the Head of Expeditions himself, together with several other important personages.

Now, to cap it all, with only a few minutes to go before the end of the programme, and just as he was about to cut the winning cake with a ceremonial knife, this strange figure in an old hat and duffle coat was hurrying up the studio telling him to *mind his blade*. It was all most disturbing.

Taking a deep breath he clasped Paddington's out-stretched paw. "It *must* be tough icing if you don't want me to cut it," he said, as Paddington introduced himself. "Anyway, congratulations on winning first prize. It's a splendid cake and beautifully made."

"You must have gone to a lot of trouble," agreed John.

"Oh, I didn't go to it," said Paddington truthfully. "It came to me."

"I like the Blue Peter badge on top," said Val as she joined the group at the table. "By the way, what are you going to choose for a prize?"

Paddington looked anxiously over his shoulder while he considered the matter. "I think," he announced, lowering his voice, "I'd like a new field kitchen if I may."

"A new *field kitchen*?" exclaimed John. "Isn't it a bit late in the year to go camping? You'll freeze to death this weather."

"Oh, I'm not going camping, Mr Noakes," said Paddington, glancing even more anxiously over his shoulder. "It's for Mr Brown. He's lost his."

"What's that?" Mr Brown, at home watching his television screen jumped up from his seat. "Who says I've lost it?"

"Paddington does, Henry dear," said Mrs Brown. "*Do*

25

sit down and listen. He's telling them all about it."

"It isn't really lost," explained Paddington, reaching forward in order to tug at a large knob of icing on the cake. "It's in here."

To everyone's astonishment the front of the cake swung open in one piece almost as if it were on hinges.

"Good gracious!" exclaimed Valerie as the closing music started to play. "That's the first time I've ever seen a door in the side of a cake, let alone one made out of icing."

"When I couldn't get the cake out," said Paddington, "I left it inside and iced the oven instead."

"What a splendid idea," said Peter enthusiastically. "No wonder you thought I might damage my blade if I tried to cut it."

"Even Petra couldn't get her teeth into that," added John, amid general agreement.

As the music grew louder and the end captions began to roll across the screen everyone in the studio gathered round Paddington's cake and began talking at once.

"Bears!" said Mr Brown expressively, as the rest of the family sat back in their chairs and looked at each other.

"Paddington!" echoed the others.

Mrs Bird folded her arms. "I've said it before," she exclaimed, as the picture faded from the screen, "and now I'll say it again. That bear takes the cake!"

2

Paddington
Gets the Bird

Mr Brown picked up his morning newspaper, carefully unfolded it, and then looked round the breakfast table. "Something," he said meaningly, "is going on."

"*Going on*, Henry?" repeated Mrs Brown, exchanging glances with the rest of the family.

Mr Brown nodded. "Look at my paper," he complained, pointing to several large holes in the front page. "It looks like a doily. Something's been eating it!"

"*And* I keep hearing noises," he continued. "Twice last night I was woken up by an awful screeching sound."

"A screeching sound?" echoed Jonathan and Judy innocently.

Mr Brown lowered his paper again. "That's another thing," he said suspiciously. "Every time I say anything this morning it gets repeated. This family sounds like a lot of parrots."

He paused, for his remark seemed to have a somewhat surprising effect on the others. "Come to think of it," he continued, "perhaps I spoke too soon. Where's Paddington? I haven't seen him yet. It's not like him to be late down for breakfast."

"I expect he's seeing to Joey," said Mrs Brown hurriedly. "It's funny you should mention parrots . . ."

"Seeing to Joey?" interrupted Mr Brown. "Who on earth is Joey when he's at home?"

Mrs Brown began to look even more ill at ease. "That's just it, Henry," she said. "He isn't at home. I expect that's why he's making rather a noise."

"Joey *is* a parrot, daddy," explained Judy.

"Paddington's been minding him for the Blue Peter programme," broke in Jonathan. "John, Val and Peter have been away on their Summer Expedition."

"And everyone else has been on holiday," said Judy. "So they asked Paddington if he would look after Joey until they get back."

"Apparently they made friends with each other when Paddington went to the studios last Christmas," explained Mrs Brown. "It turned out Joey's very keen on marmalade and Paddington happened to offer him a sandwich."

Mr Brown snorted as he picked up his newspaper. "That's not the only thing he's keen on by the look of it," he said, glaring at the remains of his business page. "He's had a good nibble at my stocks and shares as well! Two weeks. I go away for two weeks and this is what happens!"

"It's really quite an honour," said Mrs Bird, the Browns' housekeeper, coming to the rescue. "I don't suppose many bears can say they've been put in charge

29

of a famous television star."

"I quite agree," said Mrs Brown decidedly. "Anyway, Joey's going back this afternoon. It's the start of the new series."

"Paddington's been invited to appear on the programme, dad," exclaimed Jonathan.

"*Has* he?" Looking impressed in spite of himself, Mr Brown lowered his newspaper again. "Er . . . what time does it start?"

Mrs Brown looked at her husband. "Five minutes to five, Henry," she said firmly. "And don't you dare be late. Paddington's had a bath especially for the occasion and he'll be most upset if we're not all home to see him."

Unaware of the drama that was going on downstairs, the subject of the Browns' discussions sat on the edge of his bed and stared mournfully round his room.

One way and another things were in a bit of a mess. Paddington was used to getting into a mess but even he couldn't remember ever having got into such a bad one quite so early in the day.

All in all he wished he hadn't thought of giving Joey's cage a special clean in readiness for its return to the television studios.

If he hadn't thought of cleaning the cage he wouldn't have upset Mrs Bird's tin of metal polish all over the carpet. And if he hadn't upset the metal polish he wouldn't have had to fetch a bowl of hot soapy water from the bathroom. And if he hadn't accidentally stepped into the bowl of water he wouldn't have knocked the vase of flowers over.

And if he hadn't had to spend so much time clearing up the mess the flowers had made he might have given more thought to Joey himself, who during all the excitement had been flying around the room dodging from one place of safety to another.

Unfortunately, what with one thing and another Paddington had been so busy he hadn't even had time to eat any of the marmalade sandwiches which he kept in his suitcase in case of an emergency, let alone keep an eye on Joey. Very reluctantly he'd had to shut the lid and push the case under the bed in order to avoid the temptation of stopping for a snack while he got down to the important task of clearing up the room before Mrs Bird discovered the state it was in.

It wasn't until he'd got the worst of it mopped up that he had been able to give his full attention to Joey's cage, and it was then that the bottom had suddenly dropped out of his world as he contemplated a misfortune by the side of which most of his past disasters seemed mere trifles. For Joey himself was nowhere to be seen!

Paddington had looked under the bed, in the wardrobe, up the chimney – everywhere he could think of – but not so much as an empty seed shuck or discarded feather gave the slightest hint as to where he'd been, let alone where he might have disappeared to.

Sitting down on the edge of his bed again Paddington stared gloomily at the empty cage. Apart from his own feelings he shuddered to think what Val, John and Peter would have to say about the matter, let alone how the eight million viewers of Blue Peter would react when they heard the news.

Paddington was late arriving downstairs that morning

and when he did finally put in an appearance even Mrs Brown was quick to notice that something was wrong, despite the fact that he had his duffle coat hood up and his hat pulled well down over his eyes.

"You know," she said, as Paddington let himself out of the house and disappeared in the direction of the market, "I think he's really going to miss Joey. He's looking most upset and he didn't touch his breakfast. All he said was that he wanted to consult Mr Gruber about something important."

Mrs Bird stared after the retreating figure of Paddington as he rounded the corner at the end of the road. "Hmm," she said ominously. "I don't like the sound of it. If you ask me that young bear's got something up his paw. Mr Brown may have been right after all – perhaps there *is* something going on!"

The Browns' housekeeper tended to view anything abnormal in Paddington's behaviour with great suspicion. She knew from past experience that an early visit to Mr Gruber's antique shop in the Portobello Road often spelled trouble, but fortunately for the sake of peace in number thirty-two Windsor Gardens not even Mrs Bird realised quite how near the truth she was, nor, for that matter, the seriousness of Paddington's latest disaster.

John glanced up at the studio clock as the big hand ticked away the remaining few seconds before the start of the programme.

In front of him the cameras moved into their opening positions, the last of the lights came on, and overhead the microphone wiggled on the end of its boom arm as the operator made a last minute check.

Exchanging a good luck sign with Valerie and Peter, who were sitting alongside, he settled into a more comfortable position.

If the first programme in a new series was something of a strain, the last few moments before it started were the worst of all, and he knew the others were probably feeling the same way.

Petra was there, sitting quietly as ever by their side. Jason was there, equally at peace. But one important member of the family was still missing – and that was Joey.

John took one more hasty look at the grubby piece of

paper in his hand and then, as the studio manager raised his hand, he turned to face the cameras. A moment later the familiar strains of the signature tune flooded the studio and the opening picture of the programme filled

34

the screen on the various monitors dotted around the floor. Blue Peter was on the air again!

John hadn't time to read the paper, but really he had no need to. He already knew it off by heart and he didn't like the sound of it at all. It had been handed in a few minutes earlier by what the commissionaire had described as a "young, furry gentleman with a duffle coat and a large cage".

The note was short and to the point. It simply said:
DEER MR NOAKES. SORRY I AM LAIT. I AM GOING TO HAVE A BIT OF AN EMER-GENSY. SINED PADINGTON.

There was a special paw mark at the end to show it was genuine, but the thing that worried John was that if Paddington had delivered the note himself – and from the commissionaire's description it must have been Paddington – then why hadn't he come into the studio, and how did he know he was going to have an emergency anyway?

Strictly speaking Paddington ought to have turned up for the run-through earlier in the day. The lighting engineer had complained bitterly when he'd been told he had to light a cage that wasn't there, and even John, Val and Peter had felt rather silly rehearsing with a non-existent bird.

Fortunately for John's peace of mind most of the programme was taken up by the film they had made over their holiday and so once all the "hello's" had been said and the item introduced they were able to sit back and await developments.

As it happened they weren't kept waiting long, for hardly had the film got under way than there was a commotion at the door leading to the studio and a

familiar figure in a duffle coat and hat entered carrying a suitcase in one paw and a large cage covered by a cloth in the other.

"I'm sorry I'm late everyone," called Paddington, as he hurried up the studio.

"Thank goodness you've come," said Valerie, looking most relieved. "We were getting quite worried. We wondered if you'd had an accident."

"Oh, I have," said Paddington earnestly. "Lots!"

"How's Joey?" asked Peter, taking the cage.

"Joey?" repeated Paddington cautiously.

Peter lifted up a corner of the cloth and peered inside the cage. "Would you believe it?" he said. "He looks as if he's asleep."

"Come on Joey," called John, poking a finger through the bars. "Wakey. Wakey. Good old Joey!"

Paddington cleared his throat. "Good old Joey," he repeated hopefully through half-closed lips. "Good old Joey."

"Are you all right, Mr Brown?" asked Peter, anxiously.

"I'll get the studio attendant to fetch some water if you like," added Val.

Paddington looked most upset that his first effort at ventriloquism had been so unsuccessful, but before he had time to try again John broke into the conversation.

"I think we'd better get Joey's cage onto the stand," he said. "There isn't a lot of time left."

"Good idea," said Peter. "Let me have the cloth."

"I shouldn't take it off if I were you," exclaimed Paddington in alarm.

"Don't worry!" said Peter. "Besides, he'll have to get used to the lights before they come back to the studio. We don't want him flying off."

"Oh, I don't think he'll do that," said Paddington earnestly.

Whatever else he'd been about to say was lost in the gasp of surprise from those around as Peter lifted the cover off Joey's cage and they took in the sight which met their eyes.

"Joey!" exclaimed Valerie in horror. "What on earth's happened to him?"

"Good heavens!" said Peter. "He's shrunk!"

"He seems to have gone quite mouldy!" said John, peering through the bars.

"Quick," hissed the studio manager. "We're coming to the end of the film." He raised his arm in the air. "Five seconds to go . . . four . . . three . . . "

"We can't let the viewers see Joey looking like that," began John, staring at the shrivelled object inside the cage. But it was too late, the red light had already come on the camera.

37

"Well," he said, taking a deep breath as he turned to face the viewers. "That was the film we took while we were on holiday. There'll be some more next week. Now we have some news of the other members of the family. Petra, as you can see, is doing well . . . "

"And so is Jason," added Valerie.

"But we're sorry to have to tell you Joey isn't looking too well," continued John, looking rather embarrassed.

"Definitely seedy," said Peter, trying to make light of the whole affair.

"Petra-fied, you might say," agreed John, in an effort to be cheerful as a picture of the bird flashed onto the screen. He stood up and approached the cage. "Come on, Joey. Say hello!"

Taking a sidelong glance at one of the monitors John's worst fears were realised. Far from improving Joey's looks the larger-than-life-size close-up seemed to bring out his very worst features. There was a nasty looking bald patch on the crown of his head which badly needed powdering down. Part of his beak seemed to have snapped off, and altogether he looked sadly the worse for wear.

From his position on the other side of the studio even Paddington's heart sank as he peered at the picture. Joey usually looked a credit to his owners, his feathers sleek and glossy and his eyes gleaming, whereas even the most ardent admirer of the bird on the screen would have had to agree that it must at one time or another have seen better days.

However, for some reason or other Paddington seemed to view John's next remark with even more alarm. In fact, he looked so taken aback he nearly fell off his seat with surprise.

"Come along, Joey," called John. "Wakey! Wakey! Rise and shine. Show a leg there!"

Paddington picked himself up and held out a piece of wire which appeared to have several very odd looking feathers stuck to it. "I don't think he *can* show a leg, Mr Noakes," he called. "I've got it here. It came off in my paw this morning!"

The Blue Peter studio, like any other well-run television studio, was usually a model of quietness during a transmission. Even so it probably reached its quietest ever as everyone absorbed Paddington's last remark.

In this respect if was just the reverse of the lounge at number thirty-two Windsor Gardens, where the Browns sat staring disbelievingly at their screen.

"What on earth has that bear been up to now?" exclaimed Mrs Brown in dismay.

"Crikey!" groaned Jonathan. "No wonder he wouldn't let us say goodbye to Joey this morning."

"I thought it was funny the way he kept that cloth over the cage," agreed Judy.

"That *can't* be Joey," said Mrs Brown. "He *can't* have changed that much. Not in so short a time. He was all right at supper last night."

"The point is," said Mr Brown slowly, "if that isn't Joey, then where on earth can the real one have got to?"

Mrs Bird rose to her feet. "That," she announced, as Mr Brown's remark was greeted in silence, "is something I'm going to find out. Just you watch the screen and make sure that bear doesn't get up to any more mischief before I get back."

Mrs Bird didn't explain what the Browns were meant

to do about the matter if Paddington *did* get into any more trouble. Nevertheless, as the door closed behind her they turned their attention dutifully back to the screen where an unusually pale-looking Valerie was talking about doll's houses.

Interesting though the item was it received scant attention as they waited impatiently for further news of Joey, and even Valerie herself looked relieved when she came to the end. As she finished, the picture changed to a wider shot of the studio. It showed Paddington being handed a note by Peter, and, as the camera zoomed in to a closer shot of Paddington, he peered at it more closely.

"Mrs Bird wants me to eat a marmalade sandwich?" he exclaimed, reading it out loud in his surprise.

Bending down to pick up his suitcase, Paddington

began unlocking the lid. He wasn't the sort of bear to query an order which involved eating any kind of sandwich, let alone a marmalade one.

"Good," said Mrs Bird mysteriously, as she came back into the room. "I thought that might do the trick. What a good thing I got through before the programme finished."

Mr Brown stared at Paddington as if he could hardly believe his ears. "Do you mean to say the real Joey was locked in your suitcase all the time?" he exclaimed.

Paddington nodded. "That's right, Mr Brown. He must have got inside when I was cleaning my room. I I didn't see him when I shut the lid."

John had a chuckle. "I must say he gave *me* a bit of a shock when he popped out."

"Thank goodness he wasn't lost," said Valerie. "I don't know what we would have done if he had been. Apparently so many people rang up when they saw he was safe the switch-board jammed.

"Fancy putting a stuffed one in his place," said Mrs Brown. "Why ever didn't you tell us he'd disappeared?"

"I didn't like to," admitted Paddington. "Then I remembered seeing an old one in the back of Mr Gruber's shop, so I thought I'd borrow it for the time being until Joey turned up . . . " His voice trailed away. Paddington was a hopeful bear at heart but even he had to admit that now he'd said it out loud it didn't seem quite such a good idea after all.

John, Val and Peter had brought Paddington home from the studios and he was now occupying a place of honour in front of the fire alongside a very healthy looking Joey, while the rest of the family discussed the events of the day.

John gave a cough as he exchanged glances with Valerie and Peter. "I don't think we've ever awarded a Blue Peter badge to a whole family before," he said, taking a small object from his pocket, "but there's a first time for everything."

"Crikey!" exclaimed Jonathan. "A *blue* one!"

"Part of it is for Paddington," explained Valerie. "For looking after Joey while we were away."

"And the other part is for Mrs Bird," added Peter.

"After all," said John, turning to the Browns' housekeeper, "if you hadn't sent that message we might still be looking for him"

"That's a point," said Mr Brown. "What made you think of Paddington's suitcase?"

Mrs Bird looked unusually pink about the ears. "I had my suspicions when I found someone had been at my feather duster," she said. "Then when they showed that bird on television I recognised some of them. Besides," she added meaningly, "bears aren't the only ones who like marmalade! I know some birds who like it too!"

Paddington returned her gaze in amazement. It really was uncanny the way Mrs Bird 'knew' about things. All the same, strange though it was, her last remark had reminded him of something and he quickly settled back in his chair again.

Standing in the grate were some freshly toasted crumpets, oozing with butter, and he felt sure they would taste even better if they were covered with a thick layer of marmalade.

"Jolly good idea," said John, with a twinkle in his

eye as Paddington gave voice to his thoughts. "There's nothing like a jar of bear's marmalade to round things off – especially when you've only recently been 'given the bird'!"

Several loud cries of "Hear! Hear!" greeted John's remarks, but the loudest cry of all came from somewhere near the fireplace. "Joey likes marmalade," it said. "Joey likes marmalade!" And to that remark not even Paddington could find an answer.

3

Paddington
to the Rescue

Paddington peered round the Browns' breakfast table, a
large portion of bacon and eggs poised halfway to his
mouth, and stared at the rest of the family in amazement.

"We're all going to the *seaside*, Mr Brown?" he exclaimed, looking as if he could hardly believe his ears.
"In November?"

"There's a first time for everything," said Mr Brown
vaguely. "Besides, it'll set us up for the winter. A breath
of sea air will do us the world of good."

Mrs Brown gave one of her "let's change the subject"
looks. "I should have a good breakfast," she broke in.
"We've a long journey ahead of us and you ought to fill
in the odd corners."

"Anyone who's prepared to cook enough bacon and
eggs to fill in all that bear's corners is welcome," said

Mrs Bird meaningly.

The Browns' housekeeper paused at the dining-room door and looked back at the table. "And if certain people don't buck their ideas up they're liable to find themselves left behind."

A look of alarm came over Paddington's face and for the next few moments the sound of toast being crunched at high speed echoed round the room as he busied himself with his marmalade jar.

However, shortly afterwards he disappeared upstairs and after giving his whiskers a quick going-over with the flannel he turned his attention to the all-important matter of what to take with him.

Paddington had a hopeful nature and even though the barometer in the hall had been stuck at wet and windy

for over a week it was difficult not to associate the seaside with fun and games on the beach, so that by the time he made his way back down again he was pretty heavily laden.

"I hope they're all games for *one* person," said Mrs Bird grimly when she bumped into him halfway down the stairs. "Judging by the look of the weather you'll have the beach to yourself!"

Paddington looked most upset as he followed Mrs Bird's gaze out of the landing window, for apart from a bucket and spade and an inflatable rubber raft, he'd managed to collect several beach balls, a tennis racket, a fishing net, a large tyre which hung round his neck like an oversize collar, not to mention a straw hat which he'd perched precariously on top of his usual felt one; all of which seemed somewhat out of place against the leaden sky overhead.

"Never mind," said Judy, as she helped disentangle the bucket and spade from the pile. "We should never have got it all in the taxi."

"The *taxi?*" echoed Paddington, nearly falling the rest of the way downstairs in his surprise. "I've never heard of anyone going to the seaside in a taxi before!"

"It's only taking us as far as the station," explained Jonathan. "Dad's booked seats on the train."

Paddington began to look more and more mystified as he absorbed this latest piece of information. The Browns often had days out at the sea, but almost always they were very haphazard "on the spur of the moment" affairs, whereas this one seemed particularly well organised. In fact, if he'd had more time to consider the matter it might have struck him as very odd indeed.

But Paddington wasn't the sort of bear to query his

good fortune and by the time they reached the station his feeling of surprise had long since given way to one of excitement.

It wasn't often he had the chance to ride on a train and he grew even more excited as he settled back in his seat and rubbed a hole in the patch of steam on the window in order to peer out at the countryside flashing past outside. And when, some while later, Mr Brown looked at his watch and announced that they would all be having lunch in the dining-car, it practically reached fever pitch.

"I've never been in a dining-room on wheels before, Mr Brown," he exclaimed.

"Perhaps you'd like to go along and see if there are any vacant seats," said Mr Brown generously.

Paddington needed no second bidding and Mrs Brown looked at her husband nervously as there was a flurry of duffle-coat and the door to the corridor slid shut. "Do you think that was wise, Henry?" she asked.

"It's an important occasion," said Mr Brown. "We may as well let him make the most of it. Besides, if I know Paddington he won't stray very far if there's any food about."

For once Mr Brown was nearer the truth than even he imagined.

Having discovered that the dining-car itself was crowded, Paddington was about to leave when he sniffed the air several times and then turned his attention to a small hatch near the entrance. There were several interesting smells coming from the other side and by standing on tip-toe he was just able to peer over the top.

As he did so his eyes grew round with astonishment, for he found himself looking into a different world. A steamy world of hustle and bustle, of clanging pots and sizzling pans, and a chef in a white coat doing a balancing act with a pile of plates as the train rocked on its way. There were several other people hard at work and even as

he watched a waiter came dashing through a nearby door and deposited a pile of empty soup plates in the sink.

The chef looked up. "Don't take any more orders for the fish," he shouted. "It's off!"

The waiter mopped his brow. "I'm not surprised," he retorted gloomily. "Everybody's been asking for it this morning. It's one of them days. That's the way it goes. Some days it's meat. Some days it's fish."

"Good job I stepped on it," agreed the chef, stirring the contents of a large saucepan. "Otherwise some of 'em would 'ave been unlucky."

Paddington's eyes grew larger and larger as he listened to the conversation. He lowered himself down from the serving hatch with a thoughtful expression on his face, and then made his way slowly along to the dining-room itself, placing his bucket and spade on a nearby rack for safety, before settling himself on the one remaining seat at a table near the door.

As he looked round the table the thoughtful expression suddenly gave way to one of alarm.

"I shouldn't eat that if I were you," he announced, addressing the man opposite in a loud stage-whisper. "I think it's off!"

"*Off?*" The man paused, his mouth half open. "It doesn't smell too bad," he began doubtfully, applying his nose to the end of the fork. "At least . . . " He took another sniff.

Paddington looked over his shoulder. "I heard the chef tell one of the waiters," he continued knowledgeably. "He said he'd stepped on it!"

The man opposite lowered his fork and looked distastefully at the remains of his lunch. "I expect he only wanted to make it go further," said Paddington comfortingly. "They've had a rush on it."

"Really!" snorted a lady in a fur coat at the next table. She pushed her plate to one side. "I couldn't help overhearing . . . and I'm glad I did!"

Her husband nodded his agreement. "I shouldn't eat too much of *that* if I were you," he said, addressing a man further down the aisle. "The young bear gentleman with the bucket and spade saw the chef standing on it!"

In a matter of moments the dining-car was in an uproar.

"Actually jumped up and down on it, so I'm told," announced a loud voice at the other end. "It's a wonder we haven't all been poisoned."

49

A man with a large walrus moustache took up the story. "Ground it in with his heel," he snorted. "I've a jolly good mind to . . . "

Whatever else he'd been about to say or do was lost beneath a clinking of crockery and cries of "waiter" as from all sides people began calling for their bills and making their way out of the dining-car, some of them looking very green indeed.

"I must say eating on a train is very pleasant," said Mr Brown, some while later. He glanced round at the row of empty tables. "I wonder more people don't do it. It's funny we should have it all to ourselves."

The strange affair of the empty dining-car was a topic of conversation with the Browns for the rest of the journey.

Only Mrs Bird failed to join in. Not because she hadn't enjoyed her lunch, but because her eagle eyes had caught some very odd looks being cast by the staff in Paddington's direction – looks which not even a generous tip from Mr Brown entirely erased.

However, it was a very gay party of Browns who finally alighted from the train and made their way down the long hill towards the sea. Paddington in particular grew more and more excited at the prospect and he hurried on ahead of the others, waving his spade eagerly in the air.

But as they reached the promenade even his enthusiasm began to die away. A chill east wind was blowing and apart from a small group of figures who appeared to be erecting some kind of decorated stand near the pier there wasn't a soul in sight.

After testing the water he hurriedly withdrew his paw

and turned his attention to the important task of making a sandcastle. But a moment or two's digging in the cold, wet sand soon made even this pall.

Paddington stood up and surveyed his surroundings. "Perhaps I could go on the pier, Mrs Brown?" he asked hopefully.

Mrs Brown looked at him doubtfully. "I suppose he can't come to any harm, Henry," she said, turning to her husband. "I'd really like to take Jonathan and Judy shopping before they go back to school. They can go on afterwards if they want to."

"But mind you're back here by three o'clock sharp," she called out, as Paddington hurried off up the promenade. "We've something very important arranged."

Normally Mrs Brown's words would have given

Paddington food for thought, but with tenpence a week bun money burning a hole in his duffle coat pocket they fell on largely deaf ears, for he didn't want to return home again without having a go on *something* – even if it was only a chocolate machine.

The man at the turnstile eyed Paddington gloomily. "You won't find much open at this time of the year," he warned, "so don't come asking for yer money back."

Thanking the man for his information Paddington pushed his way through the turnstile and then hurried up the pier. A cold wind was blowing between the gaps in the boards and he was glad when at long last he reached the end. Looking around he began to see what the man had meant, and he rather wished he'd mentioned it before taking his threepence instead of afterwards. The large amusement arcade which occupied most of the space stood silent and shuttered, while the kiosks surrounding it were equally dark and deserted.

It was all most disappointing and he was about to turn and retrace his steps when he suddenly caught sight of an interesting looking machine standing in the shelter of a nearby doorway.

There was a picture of a large hand on the front and beneath this were the words HAVE YOUR FORTUNE TOLD – ELECTRONICALLY!

Below this there was a picture of a man inserting a fivepenny piece into a slot while placing his other hand on a large metal plate containing, so the wording underneath explained, "a thousand sensitive probes to read into your future".

Paddington wasn't at all sure what a probe was, but he read the instructions carefully several times and even though there didn't seem to be a position on the control lever marked "bears" he decided it looked very good value indeed.

In the event however, it was somewhat disappointing. Far from there being a "thousand sensitive probes" he could only count twenty-two, and most of those were so rusty they stuck halfway. For a few seconds the machine emitted a loud grinding noise and then, after a series of whirrs and clanks, a small piece of green cardboard fluttered into an opening near the base.

Paddington held the piece of card up to the light and as he did so he began to look more and more upset, for apart from the uninspiring news that his lucky colour for the day was blue, most of the space seemed to be taken up by the information that he was about to meet a dark lady bearing good tidings.

Looking around the deserted pier he couldn't see a lady of any sort let alone a dark one bearing tidings, and he was just about to throw the card away in disgust when his eye caught some wording near the bottom.

He peered at it with interest for a moment or two and then, clutching the card firmly in his paw, hurried back down the pier with a determined expression on his face.

The man in charge of the entrance didn't seem best pleased at being disturbed a second time, and he looked even less pleased when Paddington explained the reason.

"You're coming into some money?" he repeated, reading the words on the bottom of the card. "What's that got to do with me?"

Paddington held out his paw. "I'd like to come into it now, please," he announced.

The man stared at Paddington as if he could hardly

believe his eyes let alone his ears. "'ave you woken me up just to tell me that?" he demanded.

Paddington nodded. "I've only got twopence left," he explained.

The man took a deep breath. "If you go back up to the end of the pier," he said sarcastically, "you'll see a telescope. If I were you I'd bung it in there. 'cause that's what you'll need if you're going to find any money round 'ere."

Paddington gave the door to the cubby-hole a hard stare as it slammed shut in his face, then he turned and retraced his steps slowly back up the pier again in the direction of the telescope.

Putting his last remaining coin in the slot he clambered up onto the stand and applied his eye hopefully to the end.

At first everything seemed rather grey and misty, but then, as he waved it around, it began to get more interesting. All at once the horizon came into view, seemingly only a few yards away, and some of the waves against the skyline looked very choppy indeed.

Suddenly Paddington glued his eye still more tightly against the eyepiece and then he nearly fell backwards off the platform in surprise. In the middle of the lens, as large as life, a small boat had appeared.

But it wasn't so much the boat, or the way it was being tossed up and down that caused his anxiety. It was the sight of a man standing up in the bows waving his arms in a most alarming way, and even as he watched a loud cry of "Help!" reached his ears.

Paddington looked wildly about but there wasn't a soul in sight. The only sign of life came from the spot on the promenade where the workmen had been erecting the stand. For some reason or other quite a crowd seemed to have collected around it and Paddington tried waving his paws in the air, echoing the cry of "Help" from the man in the boat, but he was much too far away for it to do any good.

Without pausing to consider the matter any further he hurried across the pier and made his way down a flight of iron steps. Paddington was a brave bear at heart and it never crossed his mind to do other than go to the aid of the man in distress, but after a few moments in the icy water even he began to have second thoughts.

Apart from the fact that swimming wasn't one of his strong points, his duffle coat began to get heavier and heavier as it became waterlogged, and what with that and trying to keep his hat on with whichever paw happened to be out of the water, he soon realised that the chances of reaching the boat, let alone rescue the occupant, were very remote indeed.

A moment or so later a second cry of "Help!" broke the afternoon air. For as he turned and tried to struggle back to the safety of the pier Paddington suddenly had a nasty feeling that even this might be beyond him.

It was when he was going under for what seemed like the fiftieth time, and his struggles were growing weaker with every passing moment, that Paddington gradually became aware of a loud roaring noise in his ears.

Seconds later, though by now it all seemed part of an out-of-focus kind of dream, he heard voices and almost at once felt himself being pulled bodily out of the water.

When Paddington came round he found to his surprise that he was lying on his back surrounded by a large crowd of spectators, while a man in oilskins pulled his two front paws backwards and forwards.

"You've swallowed enough water to float a battleship," explained a voice as he opened his eyes. "Nothing to worry about, though – we're just giving you artificial respiration."

Paddington sat up. *"Artificial respiration?"* he exclaimed in alarm. Although he'd spent his last twopence he felt Mr Brown would be only too pleased to pay for the real thing if only he could be found, and he gave the man a hard stare.

At the side of the crowd Mrs Brown heaved a sigh of relief. "Thank goodness!" she said. "He's himself again."

"It'd take more than a pint or two of sea-water to sink Paddington," said Mrs Bird firmly. But even she had suspiciously red-rimmed eyes.

"What I can't understand," said Mr Brown, "is what

you were doing in the water in the first place?"

"I think I can," said the man in oilskins. "He heard me crying for help."

He turned back to Paddington. "I wasn't really in trouble," he continued. "It was all part of a demonstration."

"A *demonstration!*" exclaimed Paddington hotly. He stared from one to the other of the faces in the crowd and as he did so his eyes suddenly grew wider still, for at that moment three more familiar figures pushed their way forward.

"We're celebrating the anniversary of the launching of a new Blue Peter Inshore Rescue Boat," said Val, helping Paddington to his feet.

"As you looked after Joey so well last year," added John, taking his other paw, "we thought you'd like to come along as a special treat."

"The rescue was meant to be part of the demonstration," broke in Peter. "We didn't dream we would have to rescue you instead."

The man in oilskins stood up. "Fourteen people and a dog we've rescued so far," he announced to the crowd. "But this is the first time we've ever had to rescue a bear."

"It must have taken quite a bit of courage to jump into that water," he added, above the applause. "I don't know as I should have fancied it."

"I think you deserve a reward," broke in Valerie.

"Speech!" cried someone at the back of the crowd.

Paddington reached up in order to raise his hat to the assembly. "I don't know that I *fancied* it," he began simply. "There didn't seem to be anything else to . . ." His voice trailed away and a strange look came over his face as he began groping on top of his head.

Mrs Brown clutched her husband's arm. "Henry," she said anxiously. "You don't think he's having a relapse do you?"

"Crikey!" said Jonathan suddenly. "It's not a relapse . . . it's his hat. It's missing!"

"Quick!" shouted the man in charge of the lifeboat as the matter was explained to him. "Jump in." He led Paddington across to the waiting craft and a moment later they disappeared out to sea in a flurry of white spray.

A sigh of relief went up a moment or so later as the boat turned and headed back towards the shore, more slowly this time, with Paddington standing up in the bows waving a familiar object in his paw.

"Thank goodness for that," said Mrs Brown. "We

should never have heard the last of it otherwise."

"What are you writing?" asked John, as Valerie took out a notebook.

"Fourteen people," said Valerie. "One dog, one bear . . . and one bear's hat!"

"Not a bad record when you come to think of it," laughed Peter. "Not a bad record at all."

To that remark everyone present gave their whole-hearted agreement. And Paddington, as he stepped out of the Blue Peter Inshore Rescue Boat clutching a very bedraggled looking hat, agreed most of all.

Inside the lining he'd just come across the card bearing his fortune, and the more he considered the matter the more impressed he became. For not only had he met a dark lady bearing the good tidings of a reward, but blue had most certainly been his lucky colour for that particular day.

4

Paddington
Goes Halves

"Has anyone seen the paper serviettes?" Mrs Brown looked up hopefully from the sideboard cupboard. "It's very strange. I put a new packet here only this afternoon. Now they've gone."

"Perhaps it's the Phantom Paper Snatcher of Notting Hill Gate," said Jonathan, glancing up from his homework. "Someone's pinched my best graph paper as well."

"That's funny," broke in Judy. "I'm sure my drawing book used to be thicker."

Mrs Bird rose from behind the wastepaper basket. "If it *is* the Phantom Paper Snatcher," she said, "you might ask him what he's done with my shopping list. It's completely disappeared!"

The others exchanged mystified glances and a buzz of conversation broke out in the dining-room of number thirty-two Windsor Gardens as they began to piece together the strange jig-saw puzzle of missing items.

Mr Brown looked up from his newspaper. "I do wish you wouldn't make so much noise," he grumbled. "Anyone would think the world was about to come to an end. All this fuss about a few scraps of paper. I . . . " Mr Brown broke off suddenly as he turned a page. "Who's taken my sports section?" he demanded. "Come on, own up. Who's taken it?"

"I suppose it's a different story now?" said Mrs Brown meaningly.

"We can do without serviettes," snorted Mr Brown. "This is a serious matter. I wanted to read about the golf tournament."

"Who would do it?" he asked, looking round the room. "*Who* would possibly do a thing like that?"

"Oh crumbs!" Jonathan and Judy looked at each other.

"Quick!" said Jonathan. "Follow me."

As the Browns hurried up the stairs they none of them knew quite what to expect, but the sight which greeted their eyes as Jonathan flung open one of the landing doors drew a gasp of astonishment.

For, to say the least, the room beyond was in a state.

There was paper everywhere. Paper of all shapes, sizes and conditions. It covered the bed, the dressing table, the window sill, the chair, and even over-flowed on to the floor, where it lay in great piles and mounds like a set-piece for Doctor Who.

In the middle of it all, clutching a pair of scissors in one paw and what looked like a half-finished boat in the other, sat a familiar brown figure.

"Paddington!" cried Mrs Brown. "What on earth's

going on? I've never seen such a mess."

"A *mess*, Mrs Brown?" exclaimed Paddington, looking most offended. "It's not a mess. It's only my entry!"

"Your *entry*?" repeated Mr Brown. He gazed at the object in Paddington's paw with a marked lack of enthusiasm. Clearly visible on one of the sails was a picture

of a man carrying a golf club. "What entry?"

"I'm going in for a Blue Peter competition," Paddington announced importantly, blissfully unaware of the effect he was having. "I'm afraid I'm having trouble with my Origami!"

"Well," remarked Mrs Brown, later that evening, "we must be thankful for one thing. At least it hasn't got anything to do with glue. Paper folding may be untidy but it's clean."

"It doesn't even have to be paper," said Judy. "I watched the programme and Val said you can use anything."

"It tells you all about it here," broke in Jonathan. He picked up a copy of the Radio Times which was lying open at the Blue Peter page. "They're giving three prizes. One for the best idea. One for the best model. And one for the nost original material. It sounds jolly good."

"Mmm," said Mrs Bird ominously. "That's as maybe, but what's good for some people isn't always good for others."

The Brown's housekeeper spoke from long experience of keeping Paddington supplied with used soap cartons and old yoghourt pots, for Paddington was a keen Blue Peter fan and some evenings after Valerie's demonstrations he remained 'glued' to the television receiver in more ways than one long after the programme finished.

But for once her worst fears seemed to go unrealised, and despite the large number of half-finished models that began to appear in cupboards, heavily marked with labels like TOP SEACRET, she found little to grumble at during the days that followed.

Indeed, as time went by even Mrs Bird began to be infected by the excitement and twice she arrived home carrying a large roll of paper, while Paddington himself paid several visits to the nearby market in order to consult his friend, Mr Gruber, on the subject.

Apart from keeping an antique shop, Mr Gruber also

specialised in old books and he lent Paddington a volume entitled "A Thousand and One Things You Can Do with a Sheet of Paper".

According to the author, Mr Ivor Fold, if you armed yourself with but a single sheet of paper the world was your oyster and to prove his point the first illustration in the book showed him prising open a large model of one in order to remove a pearl.

Paddington sat up in bed for several nights carefully reading the instructions and he nearly frightened Mrs Bird to death some days later when he emerged from his room carrying the result of his efforts.

Far from looking like an oyster Paddington's model was more of a cross between an octopus and a giant marrow and when he squeezed it, instead of a pearl, the half-eaten remains of a marmalade sandwich fell out.

"I hope he doesn't try sending *that* through the post," said Mrs Brown as he disappeared down the garden. "He'll have them all out on strike."

But Paddington had other things on his mind. With the closing date of the competition drawing near a feeling of panic was beginning to come over him and as he settled himself down behind the raspberry canes with a jar of his favourite marmalade in one paw and Mr Fold's book in the other he wore a very worried expression indeed.

The models in the book grew larger and more complicated as page succeeded page and on the end-piece Mr Fold was shown climbing into an enormous space rocket made entirely of paper as he waved goodbye to his readers.

Paddington had had his eye on this particular model ever since Mr Gruber had given him the book and for the next few minutes, apart from the sound of heavy breathing and an occasional crumpling noise, all was quiet.

Mr Fold's paper was always shown neatly laid out on a table with never a mark on it, whereas looking at his own piece Paddington had to admit that it was in a bit of a mess, with earth, cabbage leaves, marmalade stains and goodness knows what else covering the surface. Apart from that, every time he unrolled it in one direction the other end followed on behind. And when he did finally manage to stand up he found himself firmly encased in a long tube utterly unable to give any kind of wave let alone a farewell one.

It was while he was struggling to release himself that he suddenly heard his name being called and he realised with a sinking heart that the Brown's neighbour, Mr Curry, was addressing him.

Mr Curry had a reputation in the neighbourhood for

being bad-tempered at the best of times and by the sound of his voice it certainly wasn't one of those.

"Bear!" roared Mr Curry. "What's going on, bear?"

Paddington took a deep breath. "It's all right, Mr Curry," he called in muffled tones. "I'm only having trouble with a join in my *Origami*."

"Go and join the army?" repeated Mr Curry. "How dare you, bear!" he spluttered. "I shall have to report you for this, I . . ."

"Not *join the army*, Mr Curry," cried Paddington desperately. "*Origami*. It's a *rocket*. I've got to finish it *today*."

"*Stop it!*" bellowed Mr Curry. "*Go away!* I most certainly will do no such thing."

Paddington struggled to his feet and peered out from the top of the tube. "Oh, no, Mr Curry," he said anxiously. "I didn't say *go away*. I wouldn't say that even though I wish you would, I mean . . ." Paddington's voice died away as he caught sight of the Brown's neighbour glaring over the top of the fence.

"I'll have you know, bear, you've ruined my afternoon's sleep," barked Mr Curry. "I demand an explanation."

"Oh, I've got one of those, Mr Curry," said Paddington, hastily launching into a long account of his activities.

Mr Curry's normally grim expression began to relax as he listened to the tale and when Paddington had finished he eyed the rocket thoughtfully.

"You say there's a prize for the best model?" he asked casually.

Paddington nodded. "I don't suppose I shall win one though, Mr Curry," he said sadly, as he clambered out of his rocket and surveyed the battered remains. "Tomorrow's the closing date for the entries and I haven't anything left to make mine with."

A crafty expression came over Mr Curry's face. "How would it be if *I* let you have some more material, bear," he asked, lowering his voice and glancing round to make sure no one else was listening. "*You* could make the model and if it wins we'll share the money."

Paddington looked at Mr Curry doubtfully. He didn't remember Valerie saying anything about there being any actual money prizes, but before he had time to explain this small matter the Browns' neighbour took hold of a loose board in the fence and held it up invitingly.

"You can use my guest room if you like, bear," he said, beckoning Paddington through the hole. "After all, you must have somewhere proper to work if we're to win a prize."

Paddington began to look more and more surprised as he squeezed through the gap in the fence and followed Mr Curry into his house.

He'd never pictured the Browns' neighbour having any guests at all let alone keeping a special room for them and he looked around with interest as Mr Curry pushed open an upstairs door.

"It's only just been decorated," said Mr Curry. "So don't make a mess. And mind the carpet. It's a new one."

Opening a cupboard he took out the remains of several rolls of wallpaper. "You can cut as much as you like off these. It's thick stuff. Just the thing for models."

"If you make a good job of it," he continued, as he made to leave, "I may even decide not to say any more about that unfortunate business outside earlier on. And no playing around. There's not much time left if you're to get it to the Television Centre by tomorrow."

Paddington stared mournfully at the door as it closed behind Mr Curry. The Browns' neighbour had a habit of twisting things round and then disappearing before anyone else had time to change their minds.

Nevertheless he was a hopeful bear at heart and rather than risk displeasing Mr Curry any further he got down to the task in hand.

Pushing the bed to one side he unrolled the paper and carefully pinned adjacent sheets of it together, fastening the ends and various other points in between to the carpet with more pins so that it didn't roll up again.

Something Mr Curry had said just before he left had triggered off an idea in the back of his mind and for the next few minutes he was kept very busy drawing lines and marking everything out, before he got down to the important matter of cutting out the exact square he was to work from.

This was the moment Paddington had been waiting for, but strangely enough he found it all much harder than he'd expected. Although Mr Curry had mentioned his wallpaper was good, thick quality he certainly hadn't expected it to be quite so difficult to cut.

In Mr Gruber's book Mr Fold usually held his paper delicately between thumb and forefinger while he snipped at it with a pair of nail scissors, whereas even kneeling down and using both paws Paddington was hard put to even make a start with Mrs Bird's scissors, let alone cut out his square.

But at long last he found himself on the homeward stretch and heaving a sigh of relief as he met up with the beginning mark on the paper, he settled himself down in the middle of the floor to enjoy a well-earned rest.

It was while he was mopping his brow with one paw and idly dipping the other into the jar of marmalade which he kept for emergencies that he suddenly caught sight of a small piece of brownish string sticking up through a slit in the paper.

Mindful of Mr Curry's warning about being tidy he carefully licked his paw clean and gave the string a tug.

It was quite a long piece of string – much longer than it had appeared at first sight, and in some strange way it seemed to be connected to other pieces, for when he came to the end a second piece popped up; only when he pulled this string it ran at right angles to the first, along the adjacent side of the square. And this, in turn, led to yet another piece.

Paddington looked more and more surprised. It was all rather like a conjuring trick; the more pieces of string he pulled the more appeared, and in no time at all he had quite a large pile by his side.

But it was when he lifted up the paper in order to investigate the matter still further that he received his biggest shock of all, and for a moment he stared at the patch of floor as if he could hardly believe his eyes.

When he'd first pinned the paper down, Mr Curry's room had been fitted with a new brown and green mottled carpet which ran from wall to wall and left not a square inch of board showing. Now he appeared to be standing on a sort of island of carpet surrounded on all sides by a small sea of crinkly brown and green waves made up of hundreds of tiny woollen tufts.

Paddington had been in some unfortunate situations before but it needed only a moment or so trying to fit the tufts of wool back on to the string and then into the gap between the two pieces of carpet to convince him that this was without doubt one of the worst he could remember, for no matter how he arranged the pile it was obvious Mr Curry's carpet would never be quite the same again.

The one bright spot on an otherwise cloudy horizon was the fact that the patch in question came where the bed had been and after picking up the square of carpet and wrapping it in the remains of the paper Paddington hastily trundled it back into place and pulled the counterpane down as far as it would go.

He was only just in the nick of time, for hardly had he got the room straight than footsteps sounded outside and a moment later the door opened and Mr Curry reappeared.

"I've been having second thoughts about this competition, bear," he announced.

"That's funny, Mr Curry," exclaimed Paddington thankfully. "So have I!"

"Ha!" Mr Curry waved a piece of paper in the air. "I had a feeling you might. That's why I brought this."

Taking an ink pad from an inside pocket he opened the lid and held it out in front of Paddington. "I'd like you to put your paw mark on this, bear," he said sternly. "Just to show it's genuine. Then there'll be no arguing about it afterwards."

As the familiar strains of the Blue Peter signature tune filled the air Mr Curry pulled up Mr Brown's best armchair and settled himself down in front of the television. "Would someone pass me the sandwiches," he called. "I don't want to miss anything."

The Browns exchanged glances. "You're sure you wouldn't like one of us to pop down the market and get you a cake?" asked Mr Brown sarcastically.

"No, that's all right," said Mr Curry. "I'll make do."

Fortunately Mrs Bird chose that moment to draw the curtains, otherwise even Mr Curry's thick skin might have changed colour had it got in the way of some of the looks being cast in his direction.

The exciting news that Paddington's last minute efforts had been rewarded and he was among the finalists for the top three prizes had spread like wildfire and the Browns' lounge was crowded for the occasion.

Mr Brown had arrived home early from the office. Mr Gruber had shut up his shop extra promptly, and quite a few of Paddington's friends from the market had dropped in; but the arrival of Mr Curry was something no-one had bargained for and as always his presence was tending to cast a gloom over the proceedings. A gloom which wasn't helped by the fact that the most important item in the programme was obviously being kept until the end.

"I do wish they'd get on with it," grumbled Mr Curry, reaching out and helping himself to the last remaining sandwich on the plate.

"They certainly know how to build up the tension," agreed Mrs Brown.

"There he is!" cried Jonathan, as a wider shot showed Paddington sitting on his suitcase in the middle of a small group at the far end of the studio.

Even as he spoke the picture changed to a closer shot and they had a tantalising glimpse of Paddington raising his hat to the viewers as the camera panned along the faces.

"It's a pity you haven't got colour," said Mr Curry.

"It's a pity some people haven't got their own television sets," snorted Mrs Bird, removing the empty sandwich plate.

It sounded as though she would have liked to say a good deal more but just then Valerie, John and Peter reappeared on the screen and Valerie led the way across the studio to where a large paper television camera stood at one end of a long table.

"Well, he hasn't won the prize for the best idea," said Mr Brown disappointedly, as the first of the winners was ushered up.

"Nor the best-made one," added Mrs Brown a moment later as the second prizewinner was announced, and the camera showed a beautifully made paper model of a space capsule.

"I can't look," said Mrs Bird, as Valerie consulted her list for the third time. "It's all too exciting for words."

"And now," said Valerie, "the prize for the most original material goes to . . . Paddington Brown of . . ."

The rest of Valerie's announcement was lost as a great cheer rang round number thirty-two Windsor Gardens.

"We've won!" cried Mr Curry. "We've won!"

"*We've* won?" Something in the tone of Mr Curry's voice made Mr Brown take his eyes from the screen for a moment. "What do you mean – *we've* won?"

Mr Curry waved a piece of paper aloft. "It's all here in black and white," he said triumphantly. "I supplied that bear of yours with the material in exchange for a half share in the prize – he's signed it with his own paw."

"Do you mean to say," exclaimed Mrs Bird, her voice trembling with indignation, "that you persuaded that young bear to sign away half his winnings? Why if I'd known I would have . . ."

"It was *my* wallpaper," interrupted Mr Curry. "If it hadn't been for my wallpaper he wouldn't have won. You heard what they said – it was for the most original material."

"I hope you like marmalade then," said Mr Brown, giving the others a wink. He pointed to the screen which was showing a close-up picture of Paddington's paws clutching an enormous stone jar. "That's what he's won!"

"Marmalade!" spluttered Mr Curry. "Do you mean to say I gave that bear my best wallpaper in exchange for a jar of marmalade?"

"*Half* a jar," corrected Mrs Bird. "That was the agreement."

Mr Gruber gave a cough. "There's another thing," he said. "I caught a glimpse of Mr Brown's model a moment ago and I must say it didn't look very much like wallpaper to me."

"What's that?" Mr Curry turned his attention back to the television just as John took up the story.

"It may not have qualified for the most original idea," said John.

"And I wouldn't like to say it's the best made," continued Peter. "Very good for paws, though," he added hastily. "It must have been pretty difficult doing all the folds."

"But it's certainly the most original material," said Valerie, as the camera pulled back to reveal Paddington's entry. "It's the only model of the BBC Television Centre I've ever seen made entirely out of carpet!"

"*Carpet!*" Mr Curry jumped to his feet, his eyes nearly popping out as he stared at the screen. "*He's made a Television Centre out of my new carpet!*"

Mr Brown turned to him as a familiar face appeared on the screen. "Do be quiet," he said. "Paddington's trying to say something."

"Thank you very much, Miss Singleton," said Paddington. "It would have been a lot bigger but I'm afraid Mr Curry's tufts kept falling out."

"My *tufts* kept falling out!" bellowed Mr Curry, beside himself with rage. "I'll give that bear tufts. I'll . . . I'll . . . "

"What ever made you choose carpet as a material?" Valerie asked Paddington. "It's most unusual."

Paddington thought for a moment. "Well, I didn't actually *choose* it," he admitted, glancing anxiously towards the camera. "It happened. It's really Mr Curry's."

"In that case," said Peter, "I think he ought to have a prize as well."

"Here! Here!" agreed Valerie.

"We don't usually award Blue Peter badges to grownups," said John, "but we'll put one in the post for Mr Curry today."

"A *badge!*" bellowed Mr Curry. "A Blue Peter *badge*. Pah!"

For once the Browns' neighbour seemed at a loss for words. He stood for a moment glaring at the others as they tried hard to keep from laughing and then he turned and strode out of the room.

"Thank goodness for that!" exclaimed Mrs Brown amid general agreement, as the sound of the front door being slammed echoed round the house. "Now perhaps we can watch the rest of the programme in peace."

"Oh, Lord!" Mr Brown's face suddenly dropped as he took another look at the model on the screen. "I've just had a thought. I suppose we shall have to buy him a new carpet. Even if it was an accident we can't just leave it."

"If it's the one in his spare bedroom," broke in Mr Gruber, "I may be able to help. I happen to know he bought it at a sale in the market. I'll get some more tomorrow and I'm sure I can arrange to have it invisibly mended."

"I must say," he added, "whatever it costs it'll be worth every penny just to be reminded of the look on Mr Curry's face when he saw young Mr Brown's model on the television."

"Perhaps it will teach him a lesson," said Judy.

"I doubt it," replied Mr Brown. "Some people are born that way." He began to chuckle as a sudden thought struck him. "I wonder if he would like to borrow my hacksaw?"

The others looked at him in surprise.

"Well," continued Mr Brown, as John, Valerie and Peter closed the programme and the camera began tracking in on Paddington's winning entry, "fair's fair. If Paddington's going to share his jar of marmalade the least Mr Curry can do is share his badge. He'll need a hacksaw to cut it in half!"

5

Paddington
Gives a Service

"Cut to camera one."

"Stand by, two."

"Make sure Petra's O.K."

"Get ready to cue John."

Paddington's eyes, which had been unusually big all that day, grew larger still as he settled back in his seat and listened to the staccato commands rising up around him in the Blue Peter gallery.

Sitting at home watching the programme go out week after week, smoothly, with rarely a hint of crises, it was indeed something of an eye-opener to be allowed in the "nerve-centre" while it actually happened.

Although he'd paid several visits to the studios in the past and knew only too well that what the viewer saw was really only like the smooth and highly polished tip of a

vast iceberg, with all sorts of other things going on
behind the scenes, he'd never before been invited to sit
in the holy of holies in order to watch a programme being
put together, and he grew more and more excited as he
felt the tension inside the gallery mount.

It was like some mammoth jig-saw puzzle, but with the
disadvantage that one piece in the wrong place and the
whole structure was liable to fall apart.

On the far side of the darkened room stood an array of
enormous television sets. Some relayed pictures from the
various cameras down in the studio; others were set aside
for viewing pieces of film to be shown later in the programme. Some had title captions; others were filled

with what seemed to Paddington's eyes like meaningless shapes and patterns, though doubtless they all had a purpose.

Most important of all was a screen labelled TRANSMISSION, which showed the picture being sent out to the viewers in their homes. Paddington was most impressed to think that not only were Mr and Mrs Brown, Jonathan and Judy, and Mrs Bird, seeing exactly the same picture back at number thirty-two Windsor Gardens, but that it was reaching ten million others as well.

In front of the monitor screens sat the director, and next to him the vision-mixer – changing the picture on the "transmission" screen at the press of a button. Beyond them were secretaries keeping a close eye on the timing of each item, the producer, the editor, a man in charge of all the technical equipment, and lots of other people too numerous to mention.

Paddington felt most important being a part of it all, for the man in charge of the gallery had said that visitors weren't normally allowed in at all during a transmission and that in all his experience it was the first time he could remember giving a bear permission.

If Paddington had any complaint at all it was that there was so much going on it was difficult to take it all in. He felt sure he wouldn't be able to remember half of it let alone explain the finer points when he next wrote a post-card to his Aunt Lucy in Peru, especially as he wasn't at all sure they had a radio in the Home for Retired Bears, let alone television.

In the end he decided to turn his attention to the view through a large window on his left.

Beyond the batteries of lights hanging from the studio

roof he could see the floor far below, with its cameras gliding to and fro – some on pedestals, one on an enormous crane – and the microphone booms following Val, John and Peter's every move as they made their way to the next item on the programme, watched by waiting figures on the side – make-up girls, wardrobe men and women, scene men – in fact, a whole army of "backroom" workers.

The view held Paddington's full attention for some while and it wasn't until he saw the studio manager listen intently in his ear-phones for a moment and then begin making frantic signals in Peter's direction as he came to the end of an item on light-houses, that he suddenly became aware of a change in the rhythm of the normally well-oiled "machinery" behind him, and as he turned back to the gallery his worst suspicions were confirmed.

Although the steady click-click as the vision-mixer changed pictures hadn't faltered, all was obviously not well.

Indeed, judging by the way the director was tearing his hair he was in the middle of a crisis which needed to be solved pretty soon otherwise he would finish the programme completely bald.

Paddington hesitated for a moment and then felt under his hat. Beneath the top, securely fastened by a piece of sticky tape, was a marmalade sandwich he kept for emergencies. From all that he could make out there was very much of an emergency taking place in the gallery at that moment and he was about to offer his sandwich around when he stopped in his tracks.

"It's no good, we'll have to swop items," shouted the director into his microphone. "Get a message to Peter.

Hold up a card or something . . *anything*. Tell him Ivan Lobitov's gone into hiding. We'll do the item on boomerangs first and take it from there. Best of luck everyone."

Paddington nearly fell off his seat with alarm and indignation as he took in the words.

"Ivan Lobitov's *hiding!*" he exclaimed hotly. "I don't know what Mrs Bird's going to say."

Fortunately Paddington's voice was lost amid the babble which broke out on all sides as the director barked out a fresh series of orders to cover the situation, and after giving the row of screens in front of him several hard stares he slumped back into his seat again in order to consider the matter.

Ivan Lobitov was one of the leading tennis players behind the Iron Curtain, and having him on the programme had been something of a scoop for Blue Peter. In saying that Mrs Bird would be upset by the news of his non-appearance Paddington was merely scratching the surface, for the Brown's housekeeper was only one of countless followers of the game who'd been awaiting the event with eagerness.

Indeed, Paddington had been looking forward to it no end himself. Although he'd never actually played tennis he'd several times challenged Mr Brown to a game of ping-pong and it was largely as a result of a letter he'd laboriously penned to Blue Peter that the whole affair, including his invitation to the studio, had come about.

It had all begun some weeks before when John and Peter had started an intensive course with a well-known tennis coach, taking the viewers with them step by step along the way.

To celebrate their completing the course a full-size

tennis court had been erected in the studio and the plan had been for Valerie to umpire a five-minute doubles match between Peter and "Boomerang" Barnes, the famous Australian seed, on one side and John and Ivan Lobitov on the other.

Mr Lobitov had appeared earlier in the day for rehearsals and then retired to his dressing-room, seemingly in the best of spirits, in order to rest. The news that he'd decided not to return to his own country and had gone into hiding for the time being was the kind of bombshell the staff of Blue Peter could well have done without in the middle of a programme, and Paddington's face grew longer and longer as one of the assistants filled in the details.

When she'd finished the girl read out a note of apology which had been found tucked beneath one of Mr Lobitov's rackets. On the normal course of events her words would have found a ready audience, but with problems arising every moment and time rapidly running out, she didn't exactly receive undivided attention.

Originally Peter had been going to introduce both guest players to the viewers after the match and invite Mr Barnes to demonstrate the boomerang from which he'd acquired his nickname.

As it was, the running order had been reversed and Peter had been left to do the item on his own *before* the match, leaving Valerie, John and Mr Barnes waiting anxiously on the court.

Now, despite frantic signals from the studio manager to make it last, even this desperate measure was coming to an end.

Another reason why the tale of woe didn't reach every

ear was because one pair in particular had already left the gallery.

In fact, Paddington was already halfway down the stairs outside, and as he made his way along the corridor leading to the dressing rooms he wore the kind of expression on his face that the Browns and Mrs Bird would have recognised immediately as boding ill for anyone who got in his way.

Fortunately for their peace of mind not even the miracle of television could penetrate the concrete walls surrounding the Television Centre, though as it happened their awareness of what was going on was to be delayed for only a minute or so, and for those left in the gallery there was even less time.

Paddington was a bear with a strong sense of right and wrong, and although he wasn't at all sure of what was going on, let alone why Mr Lobitov couldn't appear, he was determined to do something about the matter.

It was just as the director was about to send an urgent message through to the Presentation Department to say that the programme would be under-running by several minutes that his eye was caught by a rocking motion on one of the monitors as a cameraman tried to catch his attention.

"Good heavens!" he exclaimed. "What's that on camera one?"

For a few seconds everyone in the gallery watched in stunned silence as a strange-looking figure clad in a duffle-coat and hat and carrying a suitcase and tennis racket crossed the studio and entered the court at the far end.

Then the director came to life again. With Peter winding up his talk on boomerangs and nothing else left to follow it was a time for quick decisions and he made one.

"I don't know what's going on," he said, "but whatever it is we'll take a chance."

"Stand by camera one."

"Cue Valerie. We're coming over to the tennis after all."

If Valerie was taken by surprise at the sudden turn of events it didn't show in her face. In fact, it was a master-piece of controlled emotions, which was more than could be said for the occupants of number thirty-two Windsor

Gardens at that moment as they crowded round their television set.

"Paddington!" exclaimed Jonathan and Judy together.

"What on earth's that bear up to now?" groaned Mrs Brown.

"And what on earth's he got on underneath his duffle-coat?" added Mr Brown, catching a brief glimpse of something white. "It looks like a table-cloth."

"I don't know," said Mrs Bird grimly, as Paddington bent down to make some last-minute adjustments to his attire, "but by the look of things we shall soon find out."

While Valerie had been introducing the item from the top of her umpire's stand, Peter had made a quick change into his tennis clothes and by the time she'd presented "Boomerang" Barnes to the viewers he was in place beside Paddington.

"Shall I take your duffle-coat?" he asked politely. "You may find it a bit hot under the lights."

Paddington considered the matter for a moment. Now that he was actually in the studio he was beginning to wish he'd had time to look for a few safety pins, or even not bothered with Mr Lobitov's shorts at all, for they felt distinctly large and uncomfortable.

"No thank you, Mr Purves," he announced at last. "I may have an accident if you do!"

"In that case," said Valerie hastily, "perhaps we'd better start. Mr Barnes to serve."

The words were hardly out of her mouth when a sound like a pistol shot rang round the studio.

"Are you all right, Mr Brown?" asked Peter, helping Paddington to his feet and pointing him in the right direction as he replaced his hat for him.

"I think so," gasped Paddington. "I'm not quite sure."

Although he knew Mr Barnes was called "Boomerang" because of his quick returns Paddington hadn't expected the first one to be made via his head and he directed a hard stare across the net at his opponent.

"Fifteen love," called Valerie.

"Er . . . thank you, dear," replied Paddington, looking rather surprised that Miss Singleton was being unusually familiar.

The next few minutes seemed like a dream. Paddington was vaguely aware of figures in white dashing to and fro across his vision. As far as he could make out Mr Barnes's serves were even more deadly than his famous returns. Several times the ball passed perilously close to him as

Peter made valiant efforts to save the game and he was glad when at long last he heard Valerie announce that refreshments were ready.

"Thank you very much, Miss Singleton," he called, as he hurried across to the side-line. "I'd like an orange-squash please."

Playing tennis was obviously thirsty work at the best of times, but when it involved playing against someone like 'Boomerang' Barnes *and* wearing a duffle-coat into the bargain it was even worse and he was looking forward to a break in the proceedings.

"I'm afraid I didn't mean that sort of *juice*," explained Valerie. "It's a French word. *Deuce*. It means the score's forty all."

Paddington looked most disappointed. "*Forty all!*" he exclaimed, hardly able to believe his ears. "But I've only touched the ball once!"

"Advantage Barnes and Noakes," called Valerie, as the ball whistled past his right ear.

"Fancy using French," continued Paddington bitterly, addressing the world in general as the ball whistled past his left ear.

"Game Barnes and Noakes," called Valerie. "Paddington to serve. And we'd better make it quick," she continued. "Time's running out."

Swallowing his indignation, Paddington bent down to gather up a pile of balls in a corner near his suitcase. As he did so a strange expression came over his face. Something about the feel of his shorts made him realise that standing up again, let alone doing any sort of moving about on the court, was going to need a great deal of care indeed. That apart, picking up two balls was bad enough, but trying to grasp four or five at the same time – as "Boomerang" Barnes did with such apparent ease – was well nigh impossible with paws.

Paddington struggled for a moment or two and then, conscious of a note of urgency in Valerie's voice as she called for the game to begin and the sight of a man wearing headphones gesticulating in the direction of the studio clock, he came to a decision. Bending low over his suitcase, he spent the next few moments doing something mysterious to his racket.

When he did finally stand a gasp went round the studio for without moving from the spot Paddington raised his racket and the ball fairly hurtled across the court, rebounded from the floor, struck Mr Barnes a glancing blow on the chest, and then shot back across the net.

If Paddington paused in order to take aim again it was missed by the vast majority of the onlookers, and almost before Valerie had time to call out the score the process had been repeated.

"Thirty love!" shouted Valerie.

"Good work!" called Peter. "Keep it up!"

But there was no need for words of encouragement. Paddington not only looked as if he could keep going all night – he gave the appearance of being unable to help it.

"Forty love!" shouted Valerie. She was about to add 'Advantage Paddington and Purves', but it was too late. With a twang which set the studio ablaze with excitement the game came to an end and Peter was pumping Paddington's paw up and down like a yo-yo.

"Boy, what a combination," cried John as he and "Boomerang" Barnes leapt the net in order to offer their congratulations to the winning pair.

"One game each," said Valerie. "And I think that's a very fair result."

"Here, here," agreed John. "By golly, I wasn't looking forward to playing against Ivan Lobitov, but I reckon Ivan Paddington's twice as good. You must have been putting in a bit of practice on the Steppes."

"Oh, no," said Paddington earnestly. "But I've had one or two goes in Mr Brown's garage."

"I knew it!" Mr Brown jumped up and peered at his television screen. "He's been using the ball from my tennis trainer – the one with the elastic on. I usually hang it from the garage beam. I wondered where it had got to. He must have tied it to his racket."

"Ssh!" said Mrs Brown. "I think Mr Barnes is trying to say something."

"He's giving Paddington his boomerang," cried Jonathan. "Gosh! That's jolly sporting. Lucky beggar!"

"I know one thing," said Judy, as the rest of the cast gathered round to applaud, "he couldn't give it to a better person. Paddington'll think it's very good value. That's one thing he'll never be able to throw away."

As a chorus of groans mingled with the closing music of Blue Peter Mrs Brown stood up and glanced at the clock.

"Isn't it clever," she said, "how they always manage to finish the programme dead on time."

"It's not only clever," said Mr Brown, for once, but all unknowingly, doing the figure on the screen a grave injustice, "with Paddington around it's a miracle!"

6

Paddington
Weighs In

Paddington was most upset. Normally he was the sort of bear who took life very much in his stride, but for once things had taken a distinct downward plunge.

It all started when he arrived home late one afternoon only to find he'd missed almost the whole of a Blue Peter programme. Such a thing had never happened before, and what made matters even worse was the discovery that during his absence, Val, John and Peter appeared to have been robbed of all their savings.

Paddington hurried into the lounge of number thirty-two Windsor Gardens and switched on the television just as the programme was drawing to a close. Rather frustratingly, the sound on the Browns' receiver always came on before the picture, so he only heard the news to begin with, but as far as he could make out Val had lost nearly a pound, Peter just over that amount, and John even more.

When the picture finally appeared on the screen it showed, rather surprisingly in the circumstances, a view of a new hotel which had recently been completed not far from Windsor Gardens and which the Blue Peter team had been visiting. But interesting though it was to see somewhere he actually knew, it was the following scene that nearly caused Paddington to fall backwards off his stool in astonishment, for it was only then that the full drama of the situation was revealed.

Val was lying on a mat in front of the camera, apparently recovering from shock, though fortunately still in a fit enough state to wave goodbye to the viewers at home. Peter, who obviously intended going for help, was shown in close-up sitting astride a bicycle – pedalling like mad, though for some odd reason he didn't appear to be moving. While John, who seemed to have come off worst of all, was suspended from a metal bar by means of a rope looped round one of his ankles.

Had it been any other programme Paddington might not have taken the affair quite so much to heart, but he'd got to know the Blue Peter team so well over the years – both by watching them on the screen and through visiting the studio on several occasions and meeting them personally – that it seemed almost as if he'd witnessed his own family being robbed.

Unfortunately, he was the only one to have seen the incident. Normally Jonathan and Judy, the Browns' two children would have been there, but they were both away until the following evening. And with Mr Brown at his office, Mrs Brown busy sewing, and Mrs Bird – their housekeeper – even busier in the kitchen, there was just no one to talk to about the matter.

Even that night's paper didn't help. Paddington peered hopefully over Mr Brown's shoulder when he came across him reading it later that evening, but either the whole affair had happened too late to be included, or it had been hushed up, for it wasn't even mentioned.

All in all, Paddington decided there was only one thing for it. He would have to visit the scene of the crime in person. He was a bear with a strong sense of right and wrong, and he felt sure that even if he couldn't find the missing money he might well stumble across some kind of clue which might be of help.

As luck would have it, an opportunity presented itself the very next day. With Christmas drawing near, Mrs Brown and Mrs Bird planned to do some shopping in the afternoon, and as a lot of it was secret and to do with Paddington himself it had been decided to leave him at home for once.

Only Mrs Bird felt uneasy about the matter. Paddington had displayed no interest at all in the cold lunch she'd set out for him, which was most unusual, and she had a nasty feeling he had something up his paw.

Had the Browns' housekeeper been able to see the note he propped up against the salad bowl soon after they left she would have felt even more unhappy.

It said simple: INVESTIGAYTING ROBBERY AT THE KNEW HOTELL. BACK LAYTER. PADINGTUN.

But by that time it would have been too late to do anything anyway, for Paddington was already heading down Windsor Gardens as fast as his legs would carry him.

There was a very determined expression on his face indeed. An expression that bode ill for anyone who tried to divert him from his chosen course, and one which was still present some time later when he crossed the foyer of the building he'd seen on Blue Peter and approached a man sitting behind the reception desk.

"I'd like to register, please," he announced importantly.

The man behind the desk looked slightly taken aback. "Er . . . we do executive week-ends," he said, running his finger down a large book in front of him while he played for time, "but I'm afraid we haven't exactly geared ourselves to taking in bears yet. I am not sure if we can

find any vacancies."

"Oh, I don't want to stay a whole week-end," exclaimed Paddington hastily. "I have to get back to number thirty-two Windsor Gardens in time for dinner this evening. Mrs Bird won't like it if I'm late."

"*Dinner!*" For some reason the man raised his hands in horror at the very mention of the word and he looked round hurriedly to make sure no one else had overheard. "Are you sure you've thought the matter over? We do like out guests to be in the right frame of mind."

"Oh, yes," said Paddington earnestly. "I've been thinking it over all night. Ever since I saw what happened on Blue Peter."

"I know what went on," he added, lowering his voice, "and I've come to investigate the matter."

At the mention of Blue Peter the man seemed to have second thoughts about the situation. "Oh, well," he said, "in the circumstances I daresay we might arrange *something* for you."

He gave a slightly embarrassed cough as he looked Paddington up and down. "How many pounds did you have in mind?"

Crouching down in front of the desk so that the man couldn't see what was going on, Paddington opened his suitcase and felt inside the secret compartment.

"I think I could manage four," he said, peering into an envelope marked CHRISMAS PRESENT MUNNEY. "Especially if I go without buns for a week or two."

The man rose to his feet, rubbing his hands in invisible soap. "I can see I misjudged you," he said enthusiastically. "You're obviously just the sort of client we like to have."

Crossing the hall he led the way down a long, white

corridor lined on either side with doors.

Pausing outside one of them he removed a key from his pocket and placed it in the lock. "This is your room," he announced, throwing open the door. "If you like to leave your things here I'll take you along to see our Mr Constantine. You might like to start off with one of his pummels."

Paddington licked his lips as he was helped off with his duffle coat. "Yes, please," he announced. "I think I'd like two if I may."

"*Two of Mr Constantine's pummels!*" The man gazed at Paddington with a look of awe. "Nobody's ever managed two at one go before. Are you absolutely sure?"

"Quite sure," said Paddington firmly.

"Well, I must say sooner you than me," remarked the receptionist in tones of growing respect. "Though I should warn you, if you feel like a bath later on you'd better come and see me first. I'll give you a plug.

"We can't be too careful," he added, seeing Paddington's look of surprise. "After only a very small pummel some of our visitors find they can't get out once they're in. *We* keep the plugs just to be on the safe side."

Paddington's eyes grew larger and larger. The walk to the hotel, combined with the fact that he'd gone without lunch, had made him feel even more hungry than usual. Mr Constantine's pummels sounded very good value indeed and his eyes glistened as he followed the man into the corridor and down a long flight of stairs.

Pushing open a pair of double doors the receptionist stood to one side to allow Paddington to pass through. "I'm afraid Mr Constantine doesn't speak a great deal of English," he remarked, pressing a buzzer to signal their arrival. "But I am sure he will be only too pleased to show you the ropes."

Paddington thanked the man for his trouble. "I expect it's a bit difficult getting waiters these days," he said politely.

The ghost of a smile crossed the man's face as he made to leave. "You won't find any waiting with Mr Constantine," he chuckled. "He likes to get cracking straight away."

As the door closed behind him Paddington looked around the room with interest. He had been half expecting to find himself in a restaurant or at the very least some kind of canteen, whereas in fact, apart from a long narrow couch in the centre, the room seemed completely bare of furniture.

Mr Constantine himself was also out of the usual run of waiters. He was the largest man Paddington had ever seen – almost as wide as he was tall – and apart from the fact that his dress consisted simply of a white singlet and trousers, much of his face was hidden beneath an enormous black beard.

Ignoring Paddington's greeting he emitted a series of grunts and then lifted him up onto a couch, placing a hand like a bunch of bananas onto his head as he pushed him into a lying position.

Paddington hadn't had a meal in bed for a long time and he lay back with a pleased expression on his face while he waited for the sheets to arrive.

Suddenly, to his alarm, Mr Constantine gave vent to a loud snort, rather like a wild elephant having a spot of bother with its trunk, and before he had time to call out for help let alone make good his escape he felt his legs being caught in a vice-like grip.

The receptionist had said that Mr Constantine liked to get cracking, but never in his wildest moments had Paddington expected his legs to be playing the leading role.

"Ooooooooo!" he yelled, as his assailant began working them up and down with all the enthusiasm of a parched explorer who has just stumbled on a water pump in the middle of a sun-scorched desert. "Owwwwwwwwwww!"

"Urggggggggh!" grunted Mr Constantine, beaming all over his face. "Is good, no?"

"No!" shrieked Paddington.

Mr Constantine nodded approvingly, another huge smile dawning as he landed on Paddington's stomach. "This is better, yes?"

"Yes!" yelled Paddington, growing more and more confused. "I mean . . . no! It's . . . huh . . . huh . . . huh . . ." His voice died away in a long drawn-out gasp, for either

Mr Constantine was unable to take 'no' for an answer or his grasp of the English language fell a good deal short of the one he used on his victims.

It was all like a bad dream. The more Paddington shouted the more Mr Constantine seemed to take it as a signal that he was being called on for bigger and better efforts, though as Paddington's cries got louder and louder a look of concern gradually came over his face.

"You are not happy?" he enquired, standing back at last.

"No, I'm not!" gasped Paddington, struggling to a sitting position. "I thought you were going to show me the ropes."

"The ropes? Ah!" Mr Constantine's face cleared as though a great misunderstanding had been resolved. "You do not want more pummels? You want other things . . . right?"

Paddington nodded frantically, glad that he'd made his point at long last.

"Come!" Mr Constantine lifted Paddington off the couch and then beckoned him through a doorway into the next room. "I will show you!"

Paddington had barely staggered a couple of paces when he felt himself being picked up again.

"Hooray!" shouted Mr Constantine, as he placed him onto a rope hanging from the ceiling and began pushing it to and fro. "Good for tummy, no?"

"No!" shouted Paddington, clinging on for dear life.

"Whoooopeeeeeeee!" cried Mr Constantine, as he lifted Paddington off the rope and placed a belt round his middle. He pressed a switch. "Make you tingle, yes?"

"Yessssssssss!" shuddered Paddington, as the belt

began to vibrate.

If his experience on the couch had seemed like a bad dream his present situation was more like a nightmare. And as with a nightmare so all sense of time vanished as he found himself being carried from one machine to the next.

"Phewwww!" gasped Mr Constantine, as he lifted Paddington off some rollers and pushed him into a room full of steam. "Very hot. Good for pores!"

"Uhggggg!" shivered Paddington shortly afterwards, as he clambered out of a pool of ice-cold water. As far as he could make out his paws were beyond help of any kind, for they felt as if they had long ago become detached from the rest of his body.

How long it lasted he had no idea, but when he at last

crawled out into more normal surroundings he wasn't a bit surprised to discover it was already dark outside.

Paddington sat in the middle of the corridor for quite some time, making sure he was still in one piece, until gradually he became aware that someone was addressing him.

"You can't stay there," said a lady in a white uniform. "Someone might trip over you."

She looked down at him sympathetically. "You'd better come along with me. I'll take you to the dining-room. I expect you could do with your evening meal."

Paddington picked himself up, a look of undying gratitude filling his face as he followed the lady along the corridor, all thoughts of detective work driven from his mind for the time being.

As far as he was concerned he'd solved the mystery of how Val, John and Peter had been robbed. He felt sure that if they'd spent only a quarter of the time he had with Mr Constantine they'd probably been in no fit state to resist any kind of attack.

"I should try and get a seat nearer the television," whispered the lady as she led Paddington into a large, table-filled room. "The Galloping Gourmet's on and he's most popular – especially with some of our long-term residents. If you like to make yourself at home I'll ask the waitress to bring you a spoon."

Raising his hat, Paddington thanked the lady very much and then collapsed into a chair, stretching his aching paws as he took in his new surroundings.

To say that the Galloping Gourmet was popular struck him as being the understatement of the year. He'd never seen such a crowd round a television set before. They were positively drooling over it.

Mr Kerr seemed to be having trouble with a cheese soufflé, part of which had fallen on the floor, but Paddington only gave him a fleeting glance. He had much more important things on his mind at that moment. Despite his ordeal a pleasant warm glow had started to work its way up through his body, and already his taste buds were throbbing at the thought of the meal to come. A warm feeling of anticipation filled his mouth, for he particularly liked the sound of a restaurant where they didn't bother with the niceties of a knife and fork, and he sat up eagerly as a waitress bearing a silver tray entered the room and headed in his direction.

To his surprise, apart from a spoon and a bottle the tray was completely bare.

The spoon was a bit of a disappointment as well. He'd been hoping for something a good deal bigger. But he watched with interest as the lady opened the bottle and poured out a level measure of an orange coloured liquid.

"There you are dear," she said brightly, handing him the spoon. "Mind you don't spill any. I'm afraid they don't allow seconds."

"*Seconds!*" exclaimed Paddington hotly. "I haven't even had my firsts yet!"

"Ssh!" hissed a voice from the direction of the television set.

"Think yourself lucky you've got carrot juice," called someone else. "All *I've* had today is half a glass of hot water!"

"Don't eat it too fast," warned the waitress, picking up the tray as she turned to leave. "You don't want to get indigestion."

Paddington stared at the spoon in his paw as if he could hardly believe his eyes. The way he felt at that moment indigestion was likely to be the least of his problems. He could have swallowed his meal, spoon and all, without it even touching the sides of his throat.

"Four pounds!" he exclaimed bitterly, addressing the world in general. "Four pounds for a pummel and a teaspoonful of carrot juice!"

Slumping back in his chair he gazed mournfully round the dining-room. The trouble the Galloping Gourmet appeared to be having with his soufflé was nothing compared to the bother he was having with his stomach.

He'd never been quite so hungry in all his life and he felt very glad he'd managed to keep his hat on throughout the proceedings.

Taking it off, he reached inside the lining and withdrew a small paper parcel which he carefully unwrapped.

Shortly afterwards a steady munching sound began to fill the air.

It was a sound that seemed to have a strange effect on

the atmosphere in the dining-room. One out of all proportion to its size.

In fact, had the other occupants been included in any kind of survey, the Galloping Gourmet's viewing figures would have shown a sudden and most unexpected downward swing at that moment, as one by one they turned their attention away from the television screen and concentrated it on Paddington.

A sob broke out from someone at the back of the crowd, and several of those nearest to him, unable to bear the strain a moment longer, rose to their feet and began advancing towards him with a most unholy gleam in their eyes, but fortunately for Paddington's digestive system he was much too busy enjoying himself by then to notice.

Paddington wasn't the sort of bear to be caught napping in an emergency. As far as he was concerned he was living through one of the biggest he'd ever experienced in the whole of his life, and he remained blissfully unaware that there was an even bigger one drawing closer every moment.

The receptionist looked at Paddington sternly. "Eating marmalade sandwiches in our dining-room," he said, "is strictly forbidden."

He turned to the rest of the Browns gathered round his desk. "It's a good job you came when you did. I wouldn't have been responsible otherwise. Some of our residents were so upset they had to be put to bed early. We might well have had a riot on our hands."

"This isn't an ordinary sort of hotel, you know," he

continued. "This is a health centre. People come here to lose weight – not to put it on."

Paddington listened with growing astonishment. He'd never heard of anyone *wanting* to lose weight before, let alone actually paying for the privilege.

"It doesn't sound very healthy to me," he exclaimed, giving the man a hard stare. "Besides, I *always* keep a marmalade sandwich under my hat."

"What I'd like to know," said Mr Brown, hastily changing the subject, "is why you came here in the first place?"

Paddington took a deep breath. So much had happened in such a short space of time he hardly knew what to say.

"It all started when I was late for a Blue Peter programme, Mr Brown," he began. "The one where Val, John and Peter were robbed."

"*Robbed?*" repeated Mr Brown. He turned to his wife. "I didn't hear anything about a robbery, did you, Mary?"

"Well," Mrs Brown looked at the others uneasily. "Paddington *did* mention it, but I'm afraid I was rather busy at the time and . . ."

Judy gave a sudden exclamation as light began to dawn at last. "But it wasn't pounds *money* they lost," she broke in. "It was pounds avoirdupois. We saw it while we were away."

"Pounds avoirdu*paws!*" exclaimed Paddington. He examined his own paws with interest. "No wonder mine feel a bit funny."

Jonathan exchanged glances with his sister. "Judy means pounds weight," he explained patiently. "Val, John and Peter were so busy rehearsing on the machines all day they must have lost quite a bit."

"And judging by the state this young bear's in I'm not at all surprised," said Mrs Bird, fixing the receptionist with a gimlet eye.

"Not," she continued, turning back to Paddington, "that that's altogether a bad thing in some cases. Especially," she added meaningly, "as I happen to have prepared a particularly large dinner for tonight. I think we'd better pay the bill and leave the rest of the explanations until later. We don't want it to spoil."

Paddington pricked up his ears. Or rather he raised them as far as they would go in their present weakened condition, for Mrs Bird's words were the sweetest he'd heard for a long time.

In the circumstances he was quite happy to leave the explanations for as long as anyone liked.

"Perhaps," he said politely to the man behind the desk, "if I have an extra helping I may have to come back."

The receptionist gave a shudder, but before he had time to think up a suitable reply Paddington had disappeared.

Apart from looking forward to one of Mrs Bird's dinners he was anxious to get home as quickly as possible. Although there was still some time to go before the next Blue Peter programme he didn't want to run the risk of missing one ever again.

7

Paddington's
Good Deed

Mrs Brown parted the dining-room curtains at number
thirty-two Windsor Gardens and peered through the gap
at the wintry scene outside.

"I do hope Paddington's wrapped himself up well,"
she said with a shiver. "It's still snowing a blizzard."

Mr Brown glanced up from his evening paper. "We
have to go out as well, I suppose?" he asked. "I've been
looking forward all day to an evening by the fire."

His remark was greeted by a chorus of protests from
the rest of the family.

"I wouldn't like to be in your shoes if you don't go,
dad," said Jonathan.

"It isn't the Brownies fault it's snowing," added Judy.
"Besides, it *is* my old pack and Paddington has gone
to so much trouble with his appeal. We simply can't let

him down now."

"It's all very well for Paddington," said Mr Brown, making a last ditch stand. "He's got fur. It's going to be freezing cold in that tin hut of theirs. I know it."

Mr Brown spoke with feeling, for the occasion had to do with a jumble sale in aid of supplying some form of heating for the local Brownie pack, and if the look of the weather through the window was anything to go by he felt he would prefer to add his support after it had been installed rather than before.

Mrs Bird gave a snort as she bustled into the room and caught the tail end of the conversation. "If it wasn't for that bear," she said, "there probably wouldn't be anyone going at all on a night like this. He's been working his paws to the bone this last week. The very least we can do is support him."

And so saying she put on her coat and hat with an air of finality which brooked no argument.

Mr Brown gave a sigh as he stood up and removed his gaze from the roaring fire. He knew when he was beaten and truth to tell, despite his protests, he wouldn't have dreamed of missing the event.

For the past few days Paddington had never, ever, been quite so busy. It all began when he had one of his periodic clear-outs. Paddington usually had one just before Christmas in case he needed some extra space, and on the advice of Mrs Bird he'd taken some of his jumble along to the local Brownies.

Paddington had never been in a Brownie hut before and it had made a deep impression on his mind, for even with fur he'd never felt so cold in his life. If anything it had seemed even colder inside the hut than outside, and when he heard they were about to hold a jumble sale in the hope of providing some form of heating he had decided, without telling the Brownies themselves, to see what he could do to help.

Paddington was a popular bear in the neighbourhood and in no time at all offers of help had come pouring in from all directions. There was scarcely a trader in the nearby Portobello market who hadn't promised to give something, and what had started off as a vague idea in the back of his mind had taken on something of the proportions of a miniature Blue Peter appeal. Indeed, it had become known in the Brown household as PADDINGTON'S APPEAL, and knowing the enormous success Val, John, Peter and Lesley had with theirs each year he had high hopes of the Brownies reaching their own target.

"Anyway," said Mrs Bird, as they made ready to go, "there's no need to worry about him catching cold. The last time I saw him he looked as if he was all set for an expedition to the North Pole."

In saying that Paddington had been dressed to suit the weather, Mrs Bird certainly wasn't exaggerating. Although he was quite keen on snow he also believed in keeping as warm as possible, and he'd taken advantage of the occasion to wear some of his own jumble in order to kill two birds with one stone and saving carrying it all in his paws.

Apart from his own belongings he wore an extra pair of Mr Brown's Wellingtons over his own, several pullovers, and at least four scarves into the bargain. With his old hat pulled down over his ears and his duffle coat hood pulled down firmly over that, there was barely room for him to poke his nose through the gap let alone lift a paw to knock on the door of the hut, and it was some while before anyone came.

"How do you do?" said Brown Owl as she ushered him inside. "I don't think I know you. Have you come to enroll?"

Paddington licked his lips. It was a bit difficult to hear what was being said beneath all his layers, but as he caught the word "roll" his eyes brightened. "Yes, please!" he exclaimed in a muffled voice. "Cold weather makes you hungry."

The lady gave him an odd look as she helped him off with his garments. "What a stroke of luck," she said. "Sandra's gone down with a nasty bug at the last moment and we're really rather desperate. Tawny Owl's in a bit of a hole and she's holding a pow-wow."

"Tawny Owl's down a hole with a bow-wow?" repeated Paddington, wondering if he'd heard aright. "I hope she gets out."

A slightly glazed expression came into Brown Owl's

eyes, only to be replaced a moment later by one of faint distaste as Paddington handed her his old hat. "You certainly don't believe in taking any chances," she said. "I hope you don't suffer for it later."

"Oh, it's not all mine," explained Paddington. "Most of it's jumble for your sale."

The lady hurriedly placed the hat on a nearby table along with the rest of the belongings. "How very kind of you," she said. "You must be what we in the Brownies call a W.W."

"I'm not a W.W.," announced Paddington, peeling off his duffle coat. "I'm a bear!"

"A *bear!*" The lady gave a start. "Oh, dear. I'm afraid that puts a different complexion on things.

"A W.W.," she continued, "is what we call a Willing Worker."

"Oh, I'm very willing," said Paddington eagerly. "And I often do odd jobs for Mrs Bird."

"I'm sure you do," said the lady. "But that wasn't really what I meant. You see we haven't actually got a bear's section in the Brownies. There hasn't been much call for it in the past and . . . " Her voice trailed away as she caught the look in Paddington's eyes. Paddington had an extremely hard stare when he chose to use it; one that could be particularly disconcerting if you happened to be on the receiving end.

"Er . . . I'll just see what Tawny has to say," she exclaimed, backing away towards some curtains. "If you like to wait here a moment I'll have a word with her."

As the lady disappeared from view Paddington gazed around the room with interest. It had changed since his last visit. It was now divided into two halves by the curtains, behind which could be heard a great deal of chattering. The half he was standing in was filled with rows of folding chairs and tables piled high with items of clothing and boxes full of odds and ends, but before he had time to give it more than a passing glance the curtains parted again and another lady in uniform came forward to greet him.

"How do you do," she said, holding out her hand. "I'm Tawny."

"Are you really?" exclaimed Paddington, peering at her with interest. "I'm more of a dark brown myself."

"Brown Owl's been telling me all about you," said the lady, giving him an odd look. "I know it's all very irregular, and I'm not at all sure what Lady Baden-Powell would say, but as well as the jumble sale we're putting on a little Show tonight and the Gnomes are rather short."

"They usually are," said Paddington politely, picturing some in the Browns' next door garden. "Mr Curry's are only six inches high."

Tawny Owl took a deep breath. Brown Owl had told her that conversation with Paddington might be a bit difficult, but she hadn't expected it to be quite so hard. "I mean," she explained, "there should be six of them, but there are only five.

"We're turning the whole thing into a friendly competition," she went on, lowering her voice. "It's badge-taking night tonight. We don't normally encourage it but between you, me and the gatepost the different sections are having a friendly competition with each other to see who gets the most."

Paddington looked round carefully for a gatepost and then when he couldn't see one anywhere turned back to the lady. "How do they do it?" he whispered.

"Well," hissed Tawny, "there are lots of different ways. You can win a badge for being an animal lover, or reading books, or collecting things.

"You can even win one for cooking," she added. "You have to do things like fry a piece of bread."

Paddington nearly fell over backwards with surprise. He'd never heard of anyone actually winning a badge for a piece of fried bread before. "I'd like to go in for that!" he announced eagerly.

"Er . . . yes . . . " The lady began to look more and more uneasy, but fortunately she was saved the need for any further conversation by a loud knock at the door.

"I don't know why we're whispering," she exclaimed, drawing herself up to her full height. "That's probably the first of our guests. I'll take you behind the scenes to meet the others and then I must let them in."

"We're holding the jumble sale first," she explained, as she led Paddington through the curtains. "Then your section – the Gnomes – are putting on a little play. That's what we would like you to join in. It does so help if we have the right number. But Brown Owl will explain it all to you."

Paddington listened as if in a dream. He hadn't the slightest idea what was going on, but the news that he was about to take part in a play cheered him up no end.

In the excitement of the moment he even forgot to ask about his roll, but someone handed him a jelly to be going on with and he soon found himself in the thick of things.

Not that there was much chance of eating anything. It was only a very tiny make-shift stage and as far as he could make out practically the entire Brownie population of

London seemd to be crammed behind it.

Paddington's arrival caused even more excitement, for a lot of the Brownies knew him by sight, and it was some while before Brown Owl was able to restore order. Tawny Owl was gone for longer than expected and when she returned she looked most excited.

"You'll be pleased to know that everything's been going with a swing," she announced, holding up her hands for silence. "I've never seen so many people. I really don't know where they've all come from. We shall simply have to hold the sale in two parts. I know you must all be dying to get on with the play so I'll just say a few words to the audience and then we'll be ready to go."

With that she parted the curtains and there was a round of applause from the unseen audience on the other side.

Brown Owl turned to Paddington as she gathered the rest of the Gnomes around her. "Now, you'll be playing a fly," she said.

"A *fly?*" echoed Paddington, hardly able to believe his ears. "I've never heard of anyone playing a fly before. What do I have to say?"

Brown Owl looked at him uneasily. "It isn't actually a *speaking* part," she said. "I'm afraid you're not really on long enough. Though I daresay you could make a few buzzing noises if you want to and build the part up that way. As a matter of fact you're really supposed to fly out of the window soon after the curtain rises."

Paddington looked at her in disgust. He didn't think much of flies at the best of times, but never in his wildest dreams had he ever pictured actually having to play one.

But if Paddington was finding it hard to take in the turn of events on his side of the curtain the Brown family were finding it equally hard on theirs as they sat listening to Tawny's announcement about the change in the cast.

"Crikey!" exclaimed Jonathan. "Fancy Paddington being in a play. How on earth did he manage that?"

"I shudder to think," said Mrs Bird grimly.

"It's my old section too!" gasped Judy. "The Gnomes!"

The Browns lapsed into astonished silence as Tawny Owl stood to one side and the curtain rose to reveal a woodland glade. Then they joined in the applause as the first of the Brownies ran onto the stage.

Mrs Brown put her hand to her mouth as Paddington followed on behind. "Do you think he's all right?" she whispered.

It was the kind of question that couldn't receive an immediate answer, for Paddington seemed to be behaving in a very strange manner indeed. Clutching his plate of jelly in one paw, he hurried round the stage several times, making some very odd noises and waving his paws up and down for all the world as if he was about to take off. After a moment or two of this he made his way towards

the wall at the back where he appeared to be trying to open a window.

"What on earth's he doing that for?" grumbled Mr Brown. "It's cold enough in here already without making it worse."

"Perhaps he's hot from all the running?" suggested Jonathan.

"He doesn't know how lucky he is," murmured Mr Brown with a shiver. "I'm cold from all the sitting!"

From her position at the side of the stage Brown Owl looked even more unhappy. "I told him to build up the part," she groaned, turning to Tawny. "I didn't say anything about making a meal of it!"

Bur fortunately for everyone's peace of mind Paddington's enthusiasm wore off after a moment or two, and
after circling the stage several more times he drew up a
toadstool and sat down in order to watch the rest of the
proceedings.

All in all he was getting more and more fed up with his
part. Apart from the fact that he had nothing to say, his
paws were aching from the effort of flapping them up and
down, and as far as he could make out the window at
the back of the stage was frozen solid and likely to remain
so for some weeks to come.

He sat where he was for a while toying with his jelly
when to everyone's surprise he suddenly jumped up
again, his eyes growing larger and larger until they

nearly fell out of their sockets as he stared towards the back of the audience.

"Gosh!" Judy gave her brother a nudge as she followed the direction of Paddington's gaze. "Look!"

Jonathan's jaw dropped. "Crikey!" he exclaimed. "I don't believe it!"

As, one by one, the Brown family gave voice to their surprise, Paddington hurried towards the front of the stage, his plate of jelly falling unheeded at his feet.

He stared accusingly at a man sitting in the back row. "You're wearing my hat!" he announced.

"What do you mean . . . *your* hat?" The man shifted uneasily in his seat as all eyes turned towards him. "I've just bought it in the jumble sale. Paid threepence for it, I did!"

Paddington gave the unfortunate man one of his hardest ever stares. "*You bought my hat in the jumble sale?*" he exclaimed hotly. "For *threepence?*"

"Well it's not worth much more," said the man, holding it up for everyone to see. "Look at it! It's full of holes!"

Paddington gazed at his hat as if he could hardly believe his eyes. It had been given to him by his Uncle shortly before he left Darkest Peru for England, and despite its worn and tattered appearance it was one of his most treasured possessions. To have lost it would have been bad enough, but to have it sold almost under his very nose was little short of a disaster.

"Anyway," said the man, "if it's that important it shouldn't 'ave been left on the threepenny table along with all the other things."

He reached down and picked up a large and familiar-looking blue garment. "You'll be telling me next this wasn't for sale either."

A groan went up from the Browns as they recognised Paddington's duffle coat. "Now there'll be trouble!" hissed Jonathan.

In saying there was going to be trouble Jonathan made what proved to be the biggest understatement of the evening.

The words were hardly out of his mouth before it happened with a vengeance. In his anxiety to get his belongings Paddington tried to climb over the footlights

and stepped onto one of the bulbs by mistake. There was a loud bang and with a cry of anguish he leapt into the air and landed on his jelly.

What happened next no one, least of all Paddington, ever really knew for sure. He skidded across the stage, collided with a toadstool, made a grab for the curtains, and as they came away in his paw fell over and went rolling back down the stage again towards the audience.

As he disappeared over the edge the lights went out and Tawny Owl's voice could be heard ringing out clearly above the rest.

"Keep calm, everyone!" she called. "Keep calm!"

But her warning came too late, for by then Paddington had disappeared into a seething mass of curtains, toadstools, chairs, ropes, bits of jelly and pieces of wire, not to mention practically the entire first three rows of the audience.

It was some while before order was restored, and much longer still before the evening finally came to an end.

Although the other items that followed didn't lack for applause it was generally agreed that the Gnomes were the high spot of the show, and with everyone in great good humour the second half of the jumble sale was even more successful than the first; though it was noticeable that having retrieved his duffle coat and hat Paddington took care to wear them for the rest of his stay.

Being first on the scene at the time of his accident, Judy's old section won the lion's share of the proficiency badges. There were several for first aid, two needlework badges for repairing the curtains in record time, and quite a number for being animal lovers. As Tawny Owl put it during her closing speech, they were really only meant to be given to those who took care of a pet for three months, but one evening with Paddington was more than sufficient.

Paddington looked most offended at this last remark,

but he brightened considerably as he listened to the rest of the speech.

"I've been hearing all about this young bear's efforts on our behalf," said Tawny Owl, as she presented Paddington with a special "Collectors" badge of his own, "and I must say we're very lucky in our friends. We've not only made enough money out of our jumble sale to pay for the heating to be put in but we've enough left over to run it for several winters to come.

"I really think," she concluded, amid general applause, "we ought to thank both Paddington and our lucky stars for a most successful evening!"

As the Browns made their way home shortly afterwards Judy took hold of Paddington's paw. "I wonder what they're called?" she said. "Your lucky stars, I mean. It would be nice to know their names."

Paddington paused for a moment and peered thoughtfully up at the sky. "I think," he said at last, "they're probably called Val, John, Peter and Lesley. After all, if I hadn't seen all their Blue Peter appeals I don't suppose I would ever have thought of running one myself!"

The MS READ-a-thon needs young readers!

Boys and girls between 6 and 14 can join the MS READ-a-thon and help find a cure for Multiple Sclerosis by reading books. And they get two rewards — the enjoyment of reading, and the great feeling that comes from helping others.

Parents and educators: For complete information call your local MS chapter, or call toll-free (800) 243-6000. Or mail the coupon below.

Kids can help, too!